Harehound

An Existential Fable

by

Gary M. Koeppel

Coast Publishing

Editing and electronic production by
Roger W. Rybkowski | www.myadpartner.biz
Some photographs courtesy The National Greyhound Adoption Program (www.ngap.org)
Photograph page 123 copyright David Lee

LIBRARY OF CONGRESS CATALOGING IN PUBLICATION DATA

ISBN: 978-1-938924-07-1
LCCN: 2012948075

Coast Publishing

P.O. Box 223519, Carmel, California 93922
800-875-1757 • www.cstpub.com

CHAPTER ONE

The bell clamored and, before the doors were fully open, I sprang from the starting trap:

My forefeet firmly grasped the soft dirt track, my hind feet pushed forward with unquestioning strength. My spine arched and straightened with each stride and with increasing ease until my gait became the fluid essence of my forward motion, until I became the very rhythm of my advancing self.

As I became aware of the tight girth straps rubbing against my chest and underbelly, I recalled with pride how boldly the white numeral three stood out from my red jacket. Around me the pack of hounds jockeyed back and forth, each one straining forward and vying for the best positions before the pace was set. For the time being I settled comfortably in the fourth position near the rail, confident that I could better myself after the first quarter turn.

"Forward Cheque" blared my name from the loudspeaker tower in the center of the infield. For the first time that afternoon I became aware of the spectators seated around and somewhat above me in the stadium. As I lifted my head, the late afternoon sun flashed directly into my eyes. Some seconds passed before I regained focus, and then I peered ahead into the dusk-thrown shadows that lay on the floor of

the oblong track where, finally, a white blur centered itself in my vision, and I began to concentrate on our quarry, the hare, who as though without effort, was running some twenty yards in front of us along the inside rail. A vague form hopping in a graceful but frantic motion between to great ears and a tiny puffed tail, the fleeing hare was the blurred essence of my confident pursuit. With the pace set, the pack settling in and the fourth position now mine without dispute, I ran forward with selfless ease, feeling wholesome and quite satisfied with my start.

As a three-year-old I had nearly two hundred chases in the coop, a third of which I had finished in the winner's circle. This season I had finally developed that mature depth of second wind unknown to the novice, and yet I'd retained the vitality so fatefully lost by the older hounds. Each draft of air burst fully in my lungs, rushing from tail tip to forepaw and filling every breathless part of me. My limbs had never felt stronger and I'd finally learned the knack of holding back until that split second when a sudden spurt of speed rallied me from as far as fifth in line to first, and that much closer to the hare.

As the pack moved halfway into the first quarter turn, an opening appeared ahead of me, then slowly widened. Perhaps I could edge slowly up the rail and gain a post, then reserve myself until the far corner…

I surveyed the pack:

The Queen of Suir, an elegant she hound of noble lineage, maintained a steady two-length lead. Her sleek black coat, already moist, gleamed brightly in the late afternoon sun as the lean but prominent muscles of her back and thighs rippled sinuously. Her stride was true greyhound, a learned and perfected gallop altered only slightly by her own personal style. She combined her fast stride with superb grace, and ran with a kind of noble fury—unlike myself who sacrificed all dignity of form for speed.

Behind her and in front of me charged old Colonel Flash, a fawn and white one-time Grand National Champion who, during the end of last season, had begun to burn out, and who now spent most of his free kennel time in a heavy heap of noisy sleep. To compensate for his age, he started too fast from the trap, lost steam with each huffing breath and, faltering late in the backstretch, usually wound up last. With his tremendous flanks lumbering just inches from my nose, it occurred to me that his plodding gallop perfectly suited his disposition, and I felt a sudden urge to nip the old dog in a friendly sort of way but, uncertain of his reaction, I held back.

To my immediate right and barely a shoulder ahead, ran Rainless the Red, a strange name that suited his temperament as well as the streaked auburn markings on his coat. An impetuous hound with barely one season's chasing, he teased everyone and was a master of practical jokes. He boasted of the day when he alone would catch the hare, tear it limb from limb, and mount its long ears on either side of his chasing jacket as trophies. Because of his reckless maneuvers while on the track and his incessant chatter while off, he sported a reputation of low esteem within the kennels. Most of the hounds simply couldn't cope with him and became offended when he would sneak up behind them and nip their tail or, while standing beside them and talking in a quiet voice, he would leak water on their foot. And yet the other hounds' huffy disapproval and avoidance of him seemed to please rather than disturb him, and his amusement always managed to unnerve them in still another way. Although he often curled my tail and made rise my withers' hair, I felt quietly envious of his frank independence and apparent freedom from the other hounds' opinions.

Bonus, a newcomer to the kennels who took pride in his handsome neck and capacious chest, ran along the rail to my left, no doubt planning to overtake the old Colonel by sprinting up on the inside. Bonus was a pleasant, athletic sort of hound, but he kept pretty much to himself, and he was one of the few hounds who stood up to Rainless the Red by feeding back whatever Red dished out.

Saint-Harry, holding the sixth and last position, was a rather stout hound and longtime friend. Harry seemed eager to prove himself, but whenever the chance arose, he always chose to sacrifice rather than assert himself; and then, almost as if in apology, he would vaguely allude to some tenet in the

Kennel Code of Honor.

As we emerged from the first quarter-turn, Bonus faltered and I saw a chance to gain his spot in the inside lane, but before he could recover his lost steps—and before I could veer across his muzzle, Colonel Flash edged toward the rail and took the inside lane himself.

Running easily again, I settled back to save myself for the third quarter-turn. The soft smell of something sweet swept suddenly upon me, and I turned my head toward the infield where whole patches of the tall green turf were swaying and shining in the sun; then I looked toward the Winner's Circle where enormous bunches of fresh flowers overflowed from their tripod stands in colorful plumes, and it made me think of how much better it would feel to chase the hare all alone on that soft infield turf than with the other hounds in the narrow lanes of this dusty track.

We approached the second turn. I recalled the long wood splinter that stuck out dangerously from the bottom rail not too far ahead. Last week it tore open my jacket, startled me into a half-step loss, and threw me into third place. I also needed to look for the recently repaired gopher hole in the second lane along the backside straightaway, a dangerous and deceptive spot that only yesterday threw out Pride and Joy for the rest of the season with a strained shoulder. Aside from that, as far as I knew, the track was in perfect condition.

A large shadow moved steadily across the infield floor and headed directly toward the pack. Without looking up I knew it was the great sputtering bird, a thing I had never gotten used to. Several times every week it appeared to hover in the air high above our heads. Although it often descended and almost touched the ground, it never landed. It seemed to swoop down upon us during a chase for the simple pleasure of once again soaring upwards and disappearing in some distant cloud. And if the loud popping noise it made were not terrible enough to our ears, the sun's reflection from its bulbous body seemed more brilliant than the sun itself, and anyone who dared look on it was turned away. But today, strangely enough, it passed as quickly as it came, its shadow slinking silently along the infield grass and over our backs, then rippling up the stadium wall, across the crowd in the bleachers, then both sound and shadow quickly disappeared.

I moved just far enough from the inside rail to pass by the splintered wood unscathed, then darted back before the ambitious Red moved in.

Again the loudspeaker reached my ear. I raised my head and caught snatches of the wrought up crowd as they flicked

past my side vision. An old woman in a red dress lay sack-heaped across her seat and an old man was waving a paper in her face; someone shouted—I heard my name—then something incoherent; then I saw a small child, smiling, but with arm raised—cocked as if waiting to throw a paper cup; three thin women, all bunched together, were clutching one another; and then I saw a young man's fist pumping wildly up and down, a woman coiled around him, her face lost in his shoulder. I saw the track attendant, the black kennel keeper called Old Smokey, who stood gripping the exit gate with two pale hands. I passed hundreds like them every race. Some hid their face while others looked away, but most just stared with silent screaming eyes as the pack of hounds dashed quickly by.

Dusk began to fall more rapidly as the late afternoon sun sank lower causing longer shadows to creep across the lanes beyond the second turn. Ahead of me loomed the distant Mountain of Hoop that was usually girded with low hanging clouds and capped with snow, but today it rose in naked pride against an almost clear eastern sky. The mountain always called to mind my trainer, Mr. Seth, and his mystery. Every weekend he went off to a camp somewhere on the mountain and, each time he returned, I scented the smell of wild things on his boots, a smell that always threw my nose into a curious fit of ecstasy, but whenever I imagined myself venturing outside the kennels to that unknown region, I always became fearful of getting lost and—after a life spent training for the chase—I could not imagine wasting sense-lessly away on some far off mountain, alone and forgotten. And so I had always decided it was better to live with what I was certain of rather than to bound off half-cocked to some unknown place on a mountain simply to quiet a curious nose.

Then the bumping began.

Not yet half way into the backstretch, the pack began to bunch together. Old Colonel Flash, his gallop now an obvi-

ous effort, slackened his pace and began to lag. Running directly behind him, I had lost several steps while daydreaming before realizing he had slowed down. I thought of skirting around his right flank and overtaking him, but at that very instant Rainless the Red, with eyes gleaming, began closing in from the outside. If he blocked off my passing lane, I would be hemmed in against the railing and be locked behind the faltering Colonel. I readied myself for the worst.

The Queen of Suir galloped two safe lengths out front, far beyond the rest of the pack's bunching and bouting. From the corner of my eye, I saw Bonus and Saint-Harry advancing slowly up the outside to make their bids for the lead. When they reached me, I'd be surrounded on three sides, triumphantly trapped! Either I acted quickly and surpassed the winded Colonel or, boxed in by the bunch, I'd shamefully follow the old dog across the finish line—a last place finish and the day's kennel clown.

There was no choice. I decided to shoot that quickly narrowing gap between the old hound and Rainless the Red. Once beyond them, given some luck and a strong rally, I could overtake the gentle Lady Suir and wind up proud leader of the chase.

I surged forward, cautiously and with good timing, but as I drew up beside the failing Colonel, without warning, Rainless the Red dashed suddenly across the open land and thrust his lean shoulder into my unsuspecting ribs. I stumbled and slammed broadside into the already wobbling Colonel.

He roared—more in surprise than fury—then bolted sideways and bounced helplessly against the inside rail. Rebounding in a fierce snarl, he charged back toward me but, to his further dismay, I slipped through the opening he had left, then cut neatly across his muzzle, and ran breast-to-breast with Red. As the heated Colonel dropped behind, he avenged himself on me: a sharp pain nipped into my tail and I quickly pulled it in.

I knew I would have an advantage at the turn, for I had the inside lane, but I no longer felt at ease. Anything could happen once the bumping began. Checking the new positions, I saw that Bonus still paced beside the Colonel, who was panting hoarsely behind me. Saint-Harry had quietly scooted up along the outside lane and now galloped across from me on Red's mischievous right flank, lining up the three of us almost breast to breast, while the lovely Lady Suir loped all alone one long length ahead.

I wondered if Red had foreseen my plan to overtake the Colonel and had rammed me on purpose, or whether the collision was a simple accident, unavoidable. Bumping was a serious matter during a chase, and Red knew it as well as every other hound, but it seemed more than pure coincidence that he was usually involved in most of them. Whole packs have been known to fall down, clawing and yowling at one another as they tumbled clumsily into tangled heaps. A hound might emerge from such a bout with a cracked brisket, a crippled paw, or any one of an infinite number of injuries that could impair or even end his chasing career—his life.

But perhaps my suspicions were unfounded. Sometimes my jaw came too easily unhinged. And, yet, if the other hounds weren't so suspicious of my white Saluki bloodline, perhaps in turn I would not be so suspicious of them. Their superstition that the hare eludes the entire pack because it can more easily detect the white greyhound always struck me a rather simple-minded thought. They, too, had their legacies of legend and pedigree. But regardless of Red's intentions, it would be better not to accuse him but to forget it, to act as if it never happened.

Under my chasing jacket, which felt quite damp by now, my coat began to itch because my skin could not breathe freely. On some days the stifling jacket was almost unbearable and I ran with only the thought of finishing early, of shaking it off before the kennel grooms got to me, and of sprinting without restraint in the open exercise field beyond the kennels outside the stadium grounds where, flopping over on my back, I would writhe on the cool grass and kick my legs freely in the air.

Then something nudged my right thigh. Turning my head, I saw Bonus trying to muzzle in between Red and myself. Slowly, and with calm determination, he was sneaking up to squeeze into the incredibly small space between Red's hindquarter and mine. His short, harsh panting grew closer and his head began rubbing up and down against my jacket. Then Rainless the Red turned, eyes white, his neck muscles standing out and, whipping his tail, he smacked Bonus on the ear.

I wanted to lurch ahead and avoid the feuding pair but held back, for if I rallied now, I'd lose my steam and burn out in the homestretch.

Bonus had dropped behind, but his retreat was deceptive. He readied for another advance, this time his revenge, and he lunged forward with his head down. As if expecting them to

move, Red side stepped with ease as Bonus missed him and thrust his shoulder into my side. I brushed against the rail, and then righted myself. Red slowed his pace and edged over toward the advancing Bonus. As the two hounds ran side by side, Red jabbed his hock sharply into Bonus' groin, then shot ahead while Bonus, gasping in pain, fell back to the rear of the pack.

Now positive that the bumping was not accidental, my first impulse was to lash out and return the same. But upon surveying the pack, I saw that Saint-Harry had taken advantage of Red's bashing of Bonus and had moved up right behind the Queen of Suir's graceful flank. I could still overtake her if I drove myself up the inside and disregarded the bumping blow, despite the fact that now I knew for certain it was not accidental.

I decided to keep the hare—not the hound—as my quarry. Glancing up, Hoop Mountain caught my eye, and the peace of it all gripped me. A bank of low clouds now formed a ring halfway to its white peak. The quiet scene acted as a proud background for the east end of the track where a tall flagpole stood beside an enormous marble sculpture in bas-relief.

Carved into a white marble slab over ten feet wide, the scene originally depicted *The Chase* and featured six truly magnificent hounds straining after the hare, but last season some vandals had smashed off the entire left side that contained the fleeting hare and only the hounds remained in the scene. The broken marble slab that contained the Hare still lay on the ground where it had fallen. It had quickly been covered by weeds and was only barely visible.

"Forward Cheque"...my name came to me vaguely from a distant loudspeaker. The stadium noise, mounting steadily as it always did around the third corner, jarred me back into the chase. The uproar never failed to inspire me. Once it even made me imagine that I could leap right over the entire pack of hounds and, landing far beyond the lead hound, pounce mercilessly upon the ever-fleeing hare.

The Lady Suir began to tire and lose ground. She had probably over-exerted herself when warding off Saint-Harry's earlier bid. Rainless the Red glanced my way and I suspected he was planning to cut across in front of me when we entered the last turn. Bonus was keeping pace with the old Colonel behind and Saint-Harry was losing ground on the outside. If the Queen of Suir continued slowing down, that would leave only Red and I to vie for the glory of the winner's laurel.

The time was ripe and I sprang forward, but either from

a soft spot on the track or from Red's calculating foot—it happened too fast to tell—without one second's warning, I stumbled.

Off balance, with no control, I lurched sideways and smacked broadside into the railing, then bounced right back again and, missing Red who was gifted with the talent of timely side-stepping, banged headlong into the unsuspecting Bonus who, groaning from the impact, pushed me off like so much useless weight; then, completely out of kilter, without one graceful movement, I lost control of my legs, which seemed to scramble in four directions, each in search of a singular freedom; and, as if predestined to his charge, the head-down Colonel Flash thundered blindly into my rump, an outrageous blow that nearly toppled him while I, thrust high into the air, saw the mountain spinning under an incomplete sky, then heard a strange and incoherent uproar issuing from the stadium crowd, and watched the pack fairly shrink into the distance behind the fleet hare's ever-bobbing tail— all this as I somersaulted three times end over end, routed a shallow trench in the track with my snout and, rolling over sideways once, I soundly rapped my head against the hard wood rail.

CHAPTER TWO

I rose up, dazed, and Hoop Mountain grew slowly out of the ground and stood far beyond but looking over me like an old friend.

The clouds had drifted from its base. And although ever-darkening shadows continued emerging from the dusk, and even though I was covered with the dry dust of the track, with my head still awhirl, I wondered if I had ever seen the Hoop Mountain with its awesome beauty more clearly.

I planted my feet carefully beneath me and pushed myself up. The stadium crowd, roaring monotonously, leaned tensely toward the pack, by now nearly at the finish line. I wanted to compose myself before trotting in, so I began walking slowly. Thankfully, nothing felt broken or out of joint, but I know that tomorrow, despite a hot water plunge and Mr. Seth's gentle hands, I would be stiff and throbbing, though probably I would be aching less from the pain than from the indignity of it all. Upon inspecting myself further, I discovered that my jacket was missing.

I saw it lying all but hidden in the shadows of the inside lane where I had fallen. As I loped back after it, I wondered again what to do about the bumping bout, but then decided to be more cautious in the future and tell the others it had been an accident. Red was probably to blame, though I really could not be sure, but either way, the damage had been done and, besides, he would make a better distant friend than a close enemy.

As I stooped to pick up my jacket and clasp it in my jaws, it felt heavy and tasted of dirt and sweat, which reassured me that even though I had fallen it had not been all in vain. I turned and began trotting in toward the finish line where Mr. Seth would be waiting with my leash and, no doubt, with great concern about my fall and any injuries sustained. The stadium floor was almost completely swamped with dark shadows, and I could not make out the order of the hounds as the pack dashed across the finish line in the distance, but I did see the once-invincible Colonel Flash lumbering laboriously far behind the rest and, for the first time, it struck and saddened me that the old hound's chasing days were nearly over.

Then a strange roar erupted from the crowd. It startled me because their interest usually dropped off immediately after the pack crossed the finish line. Not knowing what to expect, I jerked up my head and saw that the hare had not ducked into its burrow as its usual behavior at the end of a chase but, instead, for reasons unknown, and without the slightest pause in its pace, the hare continued hopping around the track. I stopped, dumb with disbelief, and the jacket fell from my jaws.

Without exception, at the end of every chase, after we stopped at the high screen behind the starting trap, our trainers stood waiting for each hound with leash in hand as the hare hopped into his burrow somewhere in an unknown place under the stadium. The creature emerged again only at the onset of the next chase. But now, for some mysterious reason, with no let up in his pace, he continued swiftly and boldly on around the track—and shortly he would be zipping past the very place where I stood!

What to do?

My position was unique. To my knowledge, no hound—other than the hounds of legend, of course—had ever confronted the hare face to face. The hare always started out before we hounds and, fleet creature that he was, he always managed to maintain his lead throughout the chase. But now, he is running on around the track without a pack of hounds behind him and he is heading right toward me.

Imagine: to meet the hare on a hound's own terms!

A movement caught my eye. I scanned the stadium floor near the finish, and then saw Mr. Seth rushing toward me

with my leash in hand.

"Forward Cheque," he shouted, waving for me to come to him.

As the hare entered the second turn (in an instant he would be flying along the backstretch, picking up speed) I heard the great sputtering bird flying low and loudly somewhere behind and above me. Mr. Seth shouted my name again, and I was suddenly fearful that either the bird coming from behind or my trainer running toward me would frighten off the hare before it even reached me. Should I obey Mr. Seth's command and return to my leash? But how could I pass up such an opportunity? Surely Mr. Seth would be elated at my having attained the thing that we had both been striving for—and all other hounds—to catch the hare. But why, then, does he call me in? Then I realized, of course, it was obvious: Mr. Seth did not see the hare coming around the track.

In a flash, I imagined that after the catch my reputation will be firmly established in the kennels, yes even the record books; the other hounds' superstition about the white hound will be dispelled once and for all and the entire white Saluki bloodline will be forever respected; Mr. Seth's patient training will be rewarded and perhaps he will even take me with him to his camp of wild things on the mountain; the stadium crowds will recognize me on sight and will call out my name excitedly with recognition and respect. I will be well known, yes, famous. I could become history, even legend, and be revered by all.

The hare raced along the backstretch.

Mr. Seth stopped calling my name and was now running rapidly toward me with my leash whirling around his wrist. I calculated the distance between him and the oncoming hare, and realized that if I stayed where I was, Mr. Seth would be upon me before the hare turned the corner and reached me. Having really only one choice, I ran toward the hare and away from Mr. Seth to the darkened shadows along the outside lane where the hare would be unable to see me until it was too late.

The hare sped into the third turn. The great bird was hovering like a menace above me, sputtering loudly, with a bright light that could expose my position to the hare but, at the same time, it excited me with the fear it might snatch the hare for itself before it reached me.

I stopped short of where the creature would spurt out of the final turn. Thinking that surprise would help my catch, I crouched near the rail, for if he saw me now he would change course and with his speed easily elude me. I glanced over my shoulder in time to see Mr. Seth trip over the leash and sprawl fitfully upon the track.

The creature came faster, closer. With my weight evenly balanced, I tensed, crouched low and waited for my prey. My legs trembled with hope but as the great sputtering bird hovered directly above, I wondered if the hare saw me.

I took one step forward and leaped at the oncoming creature.

A circle of white pain exploded in my left shoulder, my legs shot stiffly outward, then coiled beneath me and, as a great spasm of astonishment clutched hold of me, my entire body contracted into itself; then, like ripples in a water pail, wave after wave of undulating spheres of pain radiated from my shoulder to expand and extend into a world far beyond me, a world filled with the monotonous roaring of thousands of spectators in the stadium and, as the sputtering bird ascended, I felt myself leaving a diminishing world, but before falling into the ominous blackness of my shrinking self, in quiet disbelief I watched in silence as the unharmed hare continued on around the track to the safety of his burrow.

CHAPTER THREE

I awoke slowly, with effort.

A monotonous pulsation rose and fell in my head. Moist air rushed into my lungs; it tasted warm, used; breathing was all but impossible. My whole body felt drawn together as if packed and sealed in a can of fishmeal. Although some great but unknown weight seemed to be pressing down on me, I otherwise felt as light and carefree as a passing cloud. And, aside from the incessant pounding in my head, all else was numbly silent. I longed to sleep, or at least hang onto the vaporous world that enclosed me, but of their own accord, without my willing it done, my eyes slowly opened.

A small room grew hesitantly out of the darkness. I tried to ward it off, to retain the opaque mood it was replacing but, steadily, the room developed around me.

Walls appeared, a ceiling and then a floor, all cast in a diffuse purple light. I lay on my right side, alone, on a table in the center of a room.

Cabinets filled with bottles lined the wall I faced. A door with no window broke the continuity of the wall. All else was indefinite.

My eyes blinked, found focus, and then smarted. My tail began to ache as prickles of feeling began scurrying up my flank like a herd of wild vermin. The tingling dissipated for a time around my under belly, then flared up again in my shoulder and neck. A remotely familiar and very bitter taste watered in my mouth, then a sharp smell sliced into my nose, flaring my nostrils…

The kennel surgeon's room!

In panic I tried to right myself. But finding easy movement impossible, I tried drawing up my legs beneath me. Something hindered them and they fell resolutely back beside me. Then, thinking if I marshaled my strength I could coil up and rock myself off the table to the floor, I tried thrashing my legs for motion, but they merely flailed the empty air. Something was cutting into the soft skin beneath my loins and shoulders, and I became aware of the two wide belts that were strapped and firmed cinched around my brisket and underbelly. I was bound securely to the table.

Spent, I fell back, exhausted from the effort.

The chase began returning in snatches. Finally, the fragments began arranging themselves in an order. The entire start to finish played across my mind in vivid detail.

Something about the collision haunted me. Each time I drowsed, I awoke to see the hare speeding unruffled on around the track. For awhile, each time I sought for sleep, I found it, but after a fit of slumbering, sleep no longer absorbed me and I could not escape wakefulness. Upon recalling that the hare had smashed into my shoulder, I tried moving it to survey the damage, but I could not feel a thing. Suddenly I began to fear the worst. What else would explain my presence in the surgeon's room? My shoulder bone might be out of joint, if not in fact broken and, if so, my chasing days were over. But that could not be! It made no sense. I was in my prime. Disaster struck others, but never me. If I

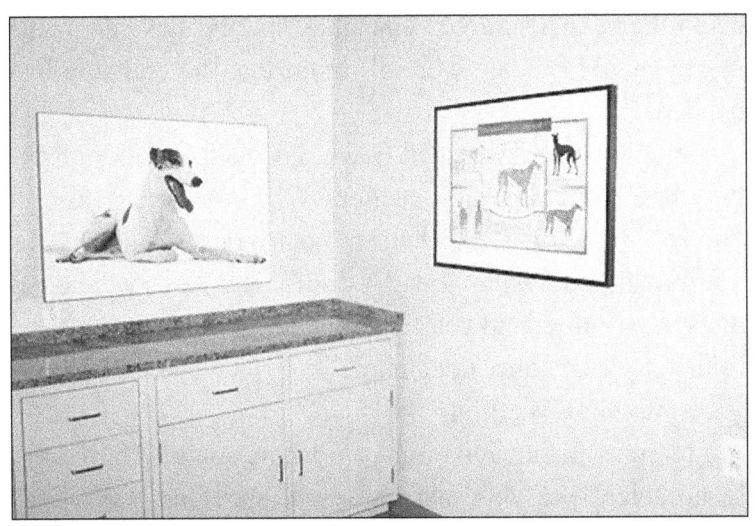

were injured, the injury simply had to be something minor.

Lights flashed in the ceiling above me and I recoiled from the brightness.

A door behind me opened, then I heard human voices. They spoke excitedly as they approached me lying on the table. I smelled Mr. Seth as his soothing hands crept under my neck. The kennel surgeon stretched open my eyes and peered into them, then busied himself with my shoulder. With one hand he pressed into the joint while, with the other, he rotated the whole leg. My shoulder came alive in spurts. The feelings increased and grew immediately into a sharp pain that slowly turned into a dull, throbbing ache.

Their presence did not comfort me. Something lingered incomplete, some thought unfinished. Again the chase flashed into my mind. The hare dashed away until out of sight, leaving me a heap on the ground. Was such a thing possible? But that was not the question. The question was about the kennel surgeon, this table, and the sickening ache in my shoulder. They were all proof that the collision had happened.

Imagine, to be smashed down, knocked senseless by—by what? That was the question: What had struck me? A powerful hare? Or a hare that was not a hare? A hare that was not a creature? A what, then? A riddle? But hares were creatures, not riddles, and yet, the thing that struck me was not a riddle, not a creature, not a hare.

It was simply a thing!

To run full tilt into some onrushing thing! And of my own choice! Had I thrown away my shoulder—my life—with less reason than if I'd tossed away an old bone? After years of training and three seasons of professional chasing, it was only a matter of time between being a rookie and certain fame, so how could I have possibly acted so foolishly?

To train and study and plan for years only to destroy it all in one silly, senseless second!

And had the other hounds seen what I had done? If so, my kennel reputation was surely now established as a hound gone mad. Yes, I had reached fame, a famous fool, and I had disgraced my entire bloodline. Now the white Saluki greyhound legend would be even more infamous and become the subject of even more ridicule and suspicion. The white hound that could not even catch the hare when chasing on his own terms! The more I thought about what I had done, the more a monstrous shame began to overwhelm me, and I forced myself to doze off into obscurity.

A different thought occurred to me when I became conscious again. Although I had not caught the hare, hadn't I

still caught a hold of something, something perhaps even more important than catching it?

It certainly was not common kennel knowledge that the hare was really a thing. The other hounds had always referred to the hare as a live creature and every hound dreamed of crossing the finish line one day with the hare hanging limply from his jaws. In fact, none of the hounds knew that the hare was a thing, a lifeless, senseless thing. Could it be possible that only I knew the truth about the hare? As the thought of my unique knowledge began to possess me, I began wanting to share it with the others. My spirits mounted and I began writhing on the table, hardly able to contain myself.

The surgeon said something and Mr. Seth laughed out-right, boldly. He leaned over, took my snoot in his hands and playfully shook my head. A moment later the kennel surgeon probed beneath me and unstrapped the belts.

I sat upright and, thinking if freedom were offered, my

legs must be sound, so I leapt from the table. But upon reaching the floor my legs buckled beneath me and I wound up in a pile skidding across the slick surface. As the kennel surgeon held open the door, Mr. Seth hefted me with a grunt and carried me from the room.

CHAPTER FOUR

The night air struck me like a whip. The dull pain in my shoulder succumbed to the stars that dazzled in the moon-struck sky above me. My excitement grew and I hoped the other hounds had not yet adjourned from the nightly kennel chats.

Mr. Seth was huffing as we entered the kennel area. It stretched along the entire length of the stadium's south wall. Individual coops were arranged in sections containing twenty hounds. An exercise yard was located in the center of each section. Since the yard was the only area lighted at night, it was there we hounds met to mingle and talk story about the day's events.

Mr. Seth laid me down gently on the mat of my coop, spoke softly for several minutes while rubbing my shoulder and then, shaking his head and sighing heavily, he left me to myself.

Once he was out of sight, I arose and strode hastily toward the lighted exercise yard. When a short distance away, I heard my name. I stopped, ears perked.

I picked out an occasional word, followed only by muf-fled sounds. Keeping among the shadows, I stole closer until the pack of hounds came into view.

Bonus stood leaning against the light pole in the center of the yard and pawed lazily at the ground; the Queen of Suir sat poised on her haunches watching Rainless the Red and Saint-Harry as they strode briskly here and there around the circle; Colonel Flash dozed on the edge of the area where the light broke off, his protruding rump was visible but his head and shoulders lay obscured in the fringe shadows; several other hounds lay scattered around the area, apparently disinterested.

The bumping bout was in hot dispute. Saint-Harry accused Red of breaking the code and causing the accident. Red fired back: since Harry had been running out front, wasn't it impossible for him to see what went on behind? Saint-Harry called on Bonus, who had been in the rear of the pack to witness the events, to comment on what he saw.

Bonus said he had not been looking.

Harry called on Colonel Flash to relate his account.

The Colonel grunted, uttered something inaudible, then returned to his dream.

Red beamed. Saint-Harry's tail drooped.

Then the Queen of Suir spoke up. In a gentle but commanding voice she declared that the bumping bouts must stop; that they had been increasing both in number and roughness lately; and that today's mishap should warn all hounds to quarrel off—not on—the track.

She finished as quietly as she began. Red started to reply, then checked himself. A timely silence fell over the group.

Limping slightly, I walked into the yard. A communal gasp arose as they spotted me. Saint-Harry bounded up to me and, without thinking, jostled against my shoulder. I winced, he pulled back, but I assured him nothing serious had come to me, and then I sat down on my haunches beside the light pole.

The Lady Suir, eyes moist, rushed toward me and rubbed her muzzle against mine. Bonus seemed genuinely pleased to see me but reserved himself. Colonel Flash, annoyed at being awakened again, heaved himself up halfway and nodded, then sank back, and at once began snoring. Rainless the Red withdrew to the edge of the yard and sprayed water against a nearby coop. Several other hounds that had been lounging around rose up, one by one, stretched and shook themselves, then stepped into the shadows and made for their coops.

The remaining hounds fell silent, their eyes darting from one to another. Finally, Saint-Harry spoke:

Exactly how did I fall?

My eyes flew to Rainless the Red who stood partly

obscured in the shadows, but to avoid his being suspected, I then looked at each of the others. The silence weighed heavier with each passing moment as I wondered how to begin. I wanted to explain about the thing, not the fall, but knew I must first set their minds at ease.

An accident, pure and simple, I replied.

The hounds all sighed relief that I had made no accusation. Red, taken aback at first, stepped confidently into the circle and grew smug.

But before they could lapse into asking the details, I asked for their silence. They sensed something more and readily complied. Hardly able to control my voice, I told them what had happened. As I spoke, even the old Colonel stirred and raised himself to listen.

I first asked if they had seen what had taken place after the bumping bout. As I suspected, as usual, immediately after crossing the finish line, they had been led through the tunnel under the stadium and then taken into the kennels. I related how the hare had continued on around the track and then, without hesitation or fear, how I had confronted and attacked the hare but, to my surprise, had been bashed senseless to the ground. Despite what we had learned and what we had always believed, I concluded, the hare was not a live creature at all and it did not hop of its own accord; instead, it was a thing, yes, merely a thing that looked and smelled like a hare, and was attached to an arm of sorts that dragged the thing around the track on the railing along the inside lane.

Now, wasn't that something?

I waited for an ensuing storm of questions, but instead was greeted with silence. They avoided my eyes and seemed

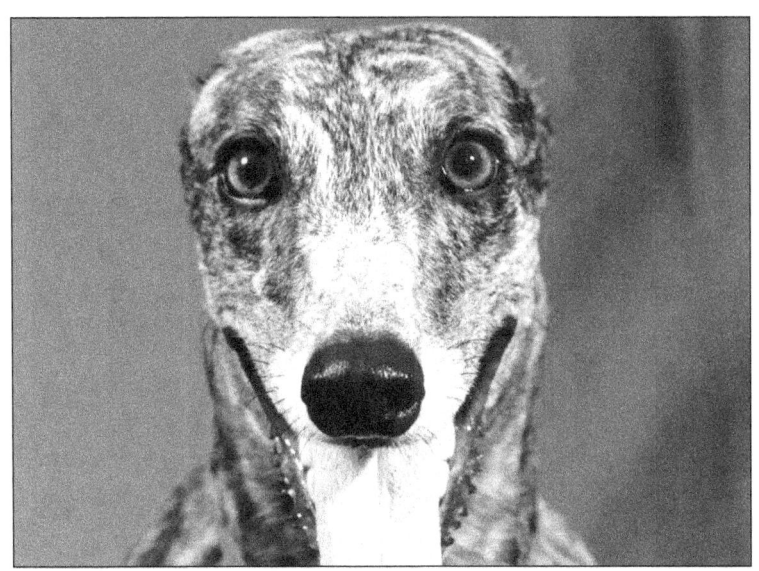

to shrink into themselves. The Colonel perked up as if to comment, but said nothing and sat down.

Well, I insisted?

Bonus excused himself and left.

Red burst out laughing.

Saint-Harry looked as if in some pain and the Queen of Suir looked away.

Only the Colonel affirmed my presence, but his glaring eyes penetrated mine so deeply I had to look away from him.

Was it that incredible, I asked?

Still nothing. Either they completely misunderstood what I had said or they thought I had gone mad. In any case, I had not expected them to react with silence, much less with ongoing silence. And the longer it continued, the angrier I became.

The hare is a thing, I repeated. It's not alive, it is a dead, mechanical thing and we are fools to keep thinking otherwise.

Saint-Harry asked if I could explain further. He said that I'd had a hard fall and perhaps, while recovering, I'd had a terrible dream. Think carefully for a moment, he implored, glancing at the others, and try to remember if I had not imagined some of what I had just said. He spoke softly, with a soothing tolerance that was to me intolerable.

I flared: I remember everything and imagined nothing. I tried to catch it—I did catch it—but it wasn't alive…

I broke off, for my anger had offended Harry. More calmly I said that what I had told them was the simple, if disturbing truth. If they had been there they would have seen it for themselves.

I then began to repeat the incident, detail by actual detail.

The Colonel roared in disapproval.

Stunned by his outburst, I fell silent. He got up and lumbered toward me, his flews curled, snorting. He denounced my words as preposterous…sheer fantasy…an excuse for falling down!

I had never seen the Colonel so worked up.

He continued saying to the rest, this young pup would sooner have us believing his fairy tale than the fact that his clumsy running cost me three posts in today's chase. But I'll have none of it! No wild story to excuse his fumbling feet, no sir!

He challenged the hounds' eyes, got no takers and stalked away growling incoherently.

Red broke into peals of taunting laughter. He hopped across the yard, imitating a hare, then shouted that something

32

had popped between my ears, then he dashed off toward his coop, hopping and staggering as he went.

Lady Suir, still unwilling to meet my eyes, excused herself with a plea of fatigue as Saint-Harry asked if he could walk with me to my coop.

I shook my head no.

Harry trudged dejectedly to the edge of the yard, then hesitated. He turned and asked if I realized the implications of my story.

I said I had thought no further than sharing it with the others.

Well, he stammered, if your story…ah…experience were true, and if the hare really was not a creature but only a thing, then the chase would be nothing more than a game. What reason then would we have to chase some mechanical thing around a track? None. Absolutely none, for we would be running around in circles with no purpose other than running around in circles. The chase would be a hoax, one grand, outrageous hoax, and everything we believed in would be false and our lives would mean nothing.

He stopped himself, said I should get some rest and that we would talk again first thing in the morning. He looked at me for what seemed a long time, then turned and vanished into the darkness.

Harry's words left me feeling as though I had just slammed head first into a closed door. Staggering from the impact, I leaned against the light pole in the center of the yard.

Given that the hare was a thing—not a creature, and that we were chasing something that was not only impossible to catch but, even if caught, would be completely useless, then yes, given these things, the chase was nothing more than pup's play—a game, a silly game of running endlessly in circles. How had Harry put it? One grand, outrageous hoax?

Black and yellow spots suddenly appeared before my eyes, shrinking and expanding. The light bulb on the pole above me had popped. Small pieces of hot glass showered down upon my coat and onto the ground around me. The dark night, as if retained in a reservoir for centuries, over-flowed into the yard.

A terrible silence engulfed the entire kennels. The still-ness seemed to be reflected in the dark expanse above me. I looked upward and my head reeled under the countless stars and enormous complexity of it all. Across the moon's face lazed an occasional cloud, whipped thin by high winds. At that moment I sensed I was the only singular thing beneath that infinite sky, and I felt more alone than the singular moon glaring down upon me.

I walked heedlessly through the broken glass that lay scattered on the ground and, as if leaving the yard for the last time, I wandered off toward my coop with the hope of leav-ing everything I had learned today behind me in the dark of night and a forgetful sleep.

CHAPTER FIVE

As I approached my coop I saw the Queen of Suir pacing back and forth. Her sleek coat gleamed as she emerged from the shadows toward me. She smiled light-heartedly, but her eyes revealed a deep concern.

A short jaunt outside the kennels, she asked?

I had no heart for sprinting. But as if sensing my thought, she explained that she merely disliked going outside the kennel area alone at night, so wouldn't I come with her?

All the other hounds were already asleep, she added.

The Queen of Suir had never failed me. Ever since I had come to the track from training school three years ago she had given me the warm concern due a hound she whelped herself. She had given me constant reassurance during the first and most difficult season. If she were in need of me tonight I couldn't possibly refuse her, though I doubted that she was really here for her own sake. More than likely she had something to say about my discovery. Perhaps she even knew something she had not wanted to reveal in front of the others.

We jogged through the quiet coops filled with sleeping hounds out into the spacious meadow nearby. Enclosed within a high wire fence, the large field was set aside for our exercise runs. Upon reaching the short grass, we broke into an easy, undemanding trot. The field rose on a gradual incline until it reached a grove of trees that lay clustered on the highest point, a knoll, which was some distance away.

The earth squeezed into my paws as we loped along. An occasional burr snagged into my coat—small headaches for the grooms who curried me before each chase. The sting-weeds rarely bothered my calloused under paws, but the strands of sharp briar that lay hidden in tangled patches throughout the field had to be watched for and averted. They could drag across one's nose and, in an instant, tear out an eye.

Colonies of droning crickets quieted as we neared them, then once again burst into song as we passed by. From time to time a mole would scamper fearfully away through the short grass and dart into some well-hidden burrow. A night bird pattered off to my left and began running in a wide circle around her nest. Grasshoppers by the dozen leaped high into the air ahead of us, as if they hoped to escape from us suspended in the air above us, but as we bore down on them, they vaulted off to the side, reaching the ground again only after we had passed by. Again the crickets' droning reached me. The chirping rose and fell in a kind of rhythmic beating, soaring gradually only to decrease and rise again, until it seemed like a pulse within me, the very breath of the field itself.

The rise became steeper as we neared the top. We stopped upon reaching the stone of Sea Foam, a gigantic boulder so named after a legendary hound who had chased and caught the hare, one of old Colonel Flash's most popular tales. I once looked upon the stone as a pinnacle of reverence, but it suddenly struck me now as being simply an absurd hunk of rock that stood for a symbol of deceit and disbelief. Panting and slightly out of breath from the run, we turned from the Sea Foam stone and lay down on the cool grass overlooking the kennels and stadium far below.

Behind me rose tall pines disturbed only by a slight breeze and, before me in the distance, lay the kennels, the place that today forever changed my life. A faint glow washed across the swaying grass in the running field. Although the night was clear and the endless stars brilliant, the air smelled slightly of rain to come. A strong smell of evergreen lingered in my nose and the pine needles poked reassuringly into my underbelly. I bit off a pinecone kernel, let it lie on my tongue, and my mouth began watering from its tart pitch.

No doubt waiting for me to speak first, the Lady Sur said nothing. Finally, unable to bear her silence any longer, I asked if she believed in what I had discovered about the hare during the chase today.

She said solemnly that she had thought about it and had tried to understand what I had said, but she simply could not bring herself to believe my story that the hare was not a creature but a thing.

The silence returned.

A great heaviness descended upon me. I looked into the field and up at the infinite night above, but its mood no longer held my interest. The Lady Sur's chin rested on her forepaws, her glazed eyes stared blankly into the valley below. I then realized that the once-strong bond between us was now abruptly something of the past. Our mutual silence of the moment spoke for itself. In her friendship I could no longer

find solace.

As if a clear but crushing blow, for the first time and now for all time, I realized that what was in my mind was mine alone.

I rose and she followed. We jogged back together in silence and soon neared the kennel entrance. She ran on ahead and, without looking back, she thanked me politely for the sprint.

The jaunt brought me neither comfort nor fatigue. Unrefreshed, I ducked under the door of my coop.

Old Colonel Flash sat inside, waiting in the outdoor exercise area of my two-room coop. A meaty T-bone hung loosely from his mouth. I walked around him and into my sleeping room where, without a word, I lay down on the mat.

He rose wearily, turned around and shuffled inside. Clearing his throat, he spoke softly, his voice broken and hardly audible. He said he understood why I was put out with him, but did I understand why he spoke out so violently about my story?

I sprang to my feet.

For a moment I couldn't speak. Then, unleashing myself, I let go of everything that had been tied up inside me since the encounter. The words, once free, flew angrily from my lips. I said that he knew as well as myself that he —not I — had made the bad, yes, the pitiful showing today during the chase. Yet, he had tried to save face in front of the others by disgracing me, by calling me a clumsy clown. He had ranted and blamed me for his own creaking legs and sagging back. He had used my story as an excuse to excuse himself; he had ridiculed me to avoid his own ridiculous showing. All this was bad, but not the worst. The worst was that he—of all the hounds, he who was the wisest hound in the kennel, our revered elder—had condemned me without even listening to my discovery.

The Colonel recoiled and the T-bone fell to the floor between his paws. Pain leaked from his eyes. I knew the truth had cut him deeply, and I checked myself.

He replied imploringly that I was right in *what* he had said, but I was wrong in *why* he had said it.

I retorted: The hare is not real. And the chase means about as much as the kennel game of Who's Got The Bone. Less, in fact, for in this game, there isn't even a bone. And we are fools to keep thinking there is.

Forward Cheque, that is precisely what I have come about, he said, sinking down on his hindquarters.

Well, then, did he think what I had said about my experience was true or not?

I know it is true, he replied soberly.

His words fell like stones on my back. I sat down. I said I did not understand.

Most hounds never discover what you have discovered today, he began. A few who have been around for years and reach a ripe old age for chasing, sometimes grow suspicious. But none of them will ever admit even the truth of their suspicions. That kind of doubt is too hard to live with anyway, so they usually forget about it as they would with any unpleasant thought.

But I, like you, discovered the truth about the hare when I was a young hound. Only the circumstances were different.

You know I am a storyteller. Most of my tales come from my head or from the hounds in my pedigree and contain little if any truth. They are just stories, tall tales for talking story. But what happened to me years ago was most unfortunately true. And it is something I will share with you if you promise me on your word of honor not to mention it to the others, ever, under any condition. Agreed?

I sighed and nodded assent.

It all happened near the end of my second season, exactly how many years ago I don't care to recall. The chase was running smoothly. I was in either second or third position. We were nearly at the finish line when the hare began to slow down, then made a strange clanking noise and suddenly it stopped dead atop the rail in the track. The entire pack was shocked to a standstill. Not knowing what else to do, we all circled around it, thinking to block off its escape, I suppose, but just exactly why I never figured out. At any rate, we stood looking dumbfounded at one another and were all wondering what to do next. Then one hound, Billy Pike, broke from the circle and jumped upon the hare. He snapped at the hare's neck, then fell back, yowling in pain.

We were all astounded. The hare had not even flinched from the attack. Baffled and growing angry, I pounced on the thing myself. I managed to tear off its head, but got only a mouthful of wood chips. Then an odd whirring sound began and, as I stood watching with its head hanging from my jaws, the thing once again began hopping slowly on around the track toward the finish line, strewing a thin trail of sawdust stuffing behind.

The Colonel spat on the ground. He paused, chewed on his lip, and looked as though he had forgotten the rest. The image of the thing trailing off shrank vividly from my mind's eye, and I shuddered in quiet but fearful expectation. The Colonel continued.

He recollected that the entire kennel was in an uproar that night. The pack had barked the news to all the other hounds. Billy Pike's jaw had been broken. Some of the hounds that had not even been in the chase demanded proof that the hare was not really a hare. When my trainer had caught and leashed me, he snatched the thing's head from my mouth and stuffed it in a pouch, so I had nothing to show the other hounds. As it turned out, though, they did not need the evidence. In fact, the very lack of it, the lack of proof, the doubt itself, was enough to destroy most of them over the next few days.

Of the six hounds in the pack I was the only one that survived. Three had gone berserk by the end of the next week, one ran away and the other was put down for distemper, although never proven that was his ailment. Several others not even in that chase shared their lot. But the remaining hounds simply began pretending that nothing had happened, nothing at all. The hounds, their trainers and keepers, and the kennel officials were soon passing off the whole thing as a terrible epidemic of distemper. We were even herded into packs to the trainer's room for shots, which I am certain was done simply to provide a reason for the debacle to other hounds in the kennel.

Well, he continued, after seeing what had happened to the others, some were my closest of friends, I decided that if I wanted to keep my own sanity, as well as the sanity of all the hounds over whom I had some influence, I would need to remain quiet and try to forget the entire incident. And, through the years, above all else, that is the single, kindest thing I have learned to do well: to keep it to yourself and forget it if you can.

I edged closer, digging my nails into the dirt floor.

The Colonel became even more intense.

If you insist on telling the other hounds, he said gravely, they will either think you have gone mad or they will believe you, which will either do you or them, or the entire kennel, irreparable harm. And if you do not forget it yourself, you will either go stark-raving mad or brood constantly and waste pitifully away. I know of only one alternative, one way, one escape. The path I have taken is to continue running in the chase: to chase *as if* the hare were real—as if there were something beyond the chase that made sense— despite the fact that we cannot understand the meaning of what that something is.

From now on you must chase with that faith hopefully in your mind and with that hope faithfully in your heart. When you have thought about it for as long as I have, you will see it is actually quite a simple, effective and, yes, even a comforting solution. For the time being, however, just remember to hold your tongue, forget the thought, and chase *as if.*

Now I've had my say. I am nearly out on my feet. I hope you have listened well. If you take it to heart, no harm will come to you or the others. But if you chose to do otherwise, well, I have nothing more to give you.

Colonel Flash heaved himself upright and shook his coarse coat. At the door, he hesitated.

Oh, yes, he said, that bone is for you. My appetite just isn't what it used to be. Besides, I don't even bury them anymore. In fact, he chuckled, I can't find them after I do.

I nodded my thanks and he all but dragged himself from my coop.

Everything that had tensed up inside me seemed to give way, to dissolve like the early morning fog. Clarity of thought returned to me as though it had never left. The formula seemed simple enough. I saw no reason why it shouldn't work for me as well as it has obviously worked for the Colonel Flash. As my esteem for the old Colonel rose, so mounted in me a sense of pride for having discovered a knowledge known by so few and for having now been taught how to cope with that knowledge.

My wits gathered together, slowly, until once again I began to feel whole. My aching limbs then drew me toward the mat and pulled me gently down.

Later that night Janice Lee, a blue-brindled she hound in heat, followed her hot nose into my coop. Her strong scent awakened me from a deep sleep. She aroused me by nipping sensually at my loin, and then groaned in extreme pleasure as I completely lost myself within her. Afterwards she wanted more, but I tumbled at once into a dreamless sleep.

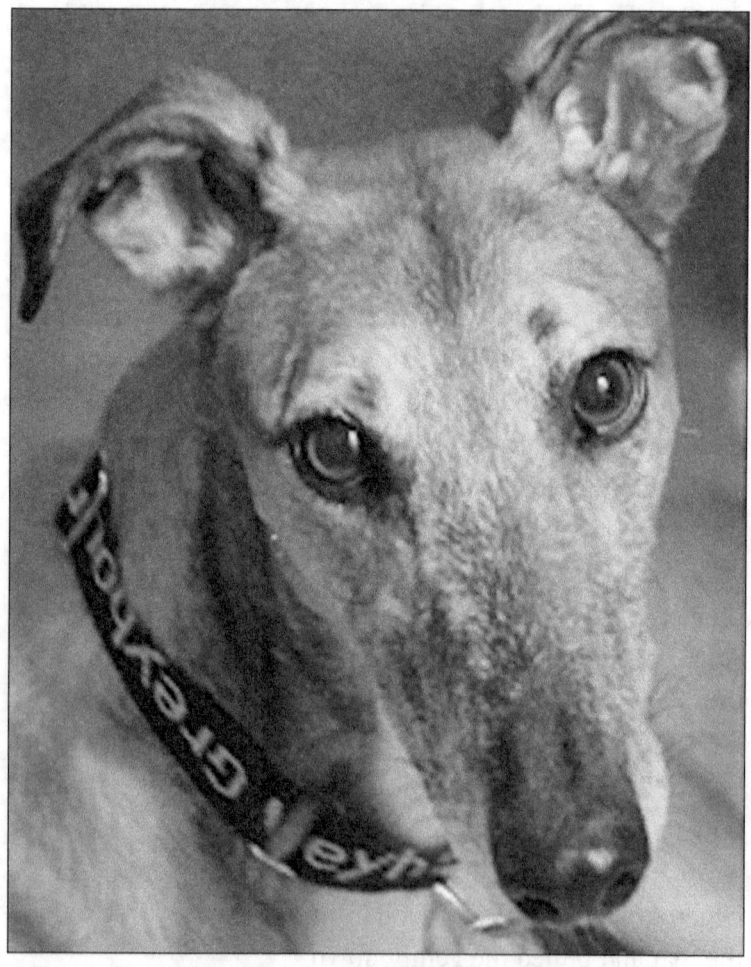

CHAPTER SIX

I awoke late, groggy:

Anxious but timid, Saint Harry stood over me with his paw poking gently into my ribs. I growled low, curled up my tail and rolled over.

You want to sleep longer, he asked?

The mat smelled of Janice Lee.

But the sun's over halfway now, Saint-Harry urged.

Why hadn't he awaked me earlier! I demanded

He cowered back, shrugging.

But I wondered why hadn't I awakened myself?

My oversleeping troubled me. I hardly ever slept after the sun rose. In fact, I usually rose just before dawn in order to take a short but unhurried sprint through the meadow. But today, with the sun almost midway in the sky, I had slept so long I might even miss the first chase.

Why hadn't Mr. Seth awakened me? Then the events of the day before tumbled into my head and a vague fear gripped me. I pressed down on my shoulder and it began to ache, dully at first, then with more and more intensity. Had Mr. Seth taken me from the day's chase because of my injury?

Saint-Harry asked doubtfully if I were feeling better.

Recalling Colonel Flash's comforting words, I assured Harry that everything had righted itself.

He shuffled nervously and looked unconvinced.

Now get along, I told him, I'll meet you in the grooming room.

Still, he hesitated.

I smacked him playfully with my tail.

That's better, he said, that's the Forward Cheque I know! Then, leaping like a pup, he bounded from my coop.

I thrust out my forelegs and, dipping my spine, I stretched until my chin lay flat on the floor. My shoulder wasn't nearly as tight as I'd expected; a little exercise would shake it loose.

I gulped down the fresh mixture of meat and fishmeal left that morning by Old Smokey, the black kennel keeper. It seemed odd that even he hadn't roused me from my sound sleep, for he usually made quite a ruckus with his tin pail and wood ladle. After lapping up some water, I stepped outside. The sun glared boldly overhead, nearly staggering me with its brilliance. The air was tepid and my coat felt damp. During the chase I expected the wet heat would be all but unbearable.

Looking around I noted that the entire kennel area was deserted. Since the hour was late, the other hounds were already in the cool grooming room beneath the stadium. If Mr. Seth had come looking for me, he would think my injury was worse than it actually was. I strode over to Rainless the Red's empty coop and, with mixed feelings, sprayed against the wall and felt relieved. Refreshed, I trotted off briskly toward the grooming room.

Emerging from the kennels and approaching the entrance, I spotted Mr. Seth walking toward me. Hoping he wouldn't notice my stiff shoulder, I jogged to him.

He seemed relieved to see me, rubbed my head

affectionately, then knelt down and began probing around my shoulder. I winced as he struck a tender spot. He withdrew, stroking his jaw thoughtfully, but seemed satisfied with the inspection. Then, smiling fully, he swatted my flank and off we went.

Leaving the hot sun behind us, we stepped into the shade beneath the stadium and went into the large, cool grooming room. Countless hounds stood in the stalls that surrounded the inner exercise area. The kennel grooms were attending to their coats, meticulously cleaning and currying them for the day's chases. A few hounds were being walked in parade around the center of the room. They had been selected to run in the day's first chase and were practicing for the opening ceremonies around the winner's circle, a ritual most hounds disliked but one I had always found inspiring.

I looked for Colonel Flash. Bonus sat in a stall on the far side of the room looking quite nonplussed as an attendant combed him with a wire brush. I passed Rainless the Red unnoticed, for he was pinned flat on the ground by the kennel surgeon who was poking a finger in his mouth. Saint-Harry sat obediently at the foot of his groom who, neglecting his duties, was waving his arms and talking excitedly to a short man who leaned passively on a cane. Harry barked a friendly greeting upon seeing me, but was squelched when the groom's toe jiggled his meaty ribs. The Queen of Suir, admiring herself in the tall, three-sided grooming mirror that stood in the middle of the room, following me with her eyes until I nodded, and only then she looked away. As we approached my stall, I realized that Colonel Flash was nowhere in the room.

Two grooms pounced upon me. One grumbled as he picked burrs from my coat and began washing me with a damp sponge. The other, a tall groom who smelled like burning straw, grasped me roughly and began pressing his long thumbs deeply into my already aching shoulder. Mr. Seth spoke to them for a time, then turned to me with a curious smile and quickly left the room

Across the aisle Lady Suir sat gracefully on her hindquarters while the groom stroked her black coat. I sensed that last night I had lost something more than a friend, something greater than a source of comfort, but exactly what that something was I didn't know. As though looking at her would show me the answer, I squinted my eyes to observe her more closely.

But she looked as she always had looked, or so it seemed:

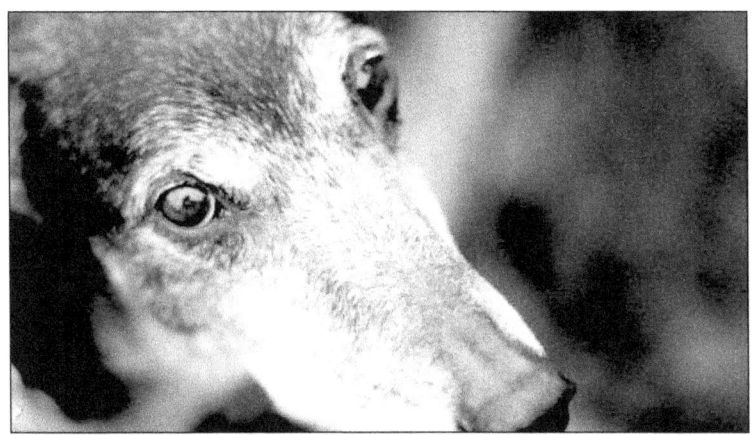

feminine, reserved, with poised dignity and at peace with the world. Yet, the longer I watched her, the more obvious became her age. Dark, deeply lined furrows surrounded her eyes. Perhaps it was due to her seated position, but her underbelly seemed to sag slightly as if she hound's in her early stage of whelping. Her black coat was not nearly as sleek as I had remembered. I supped that she had either slept badly or she had a touch of belly bugs. A lot of vermin seemed to have been crawling around the kennels lately.

Then her groom did something I had never seen before. He poured some thick liquid from a bottle into a sponge and began rubbing it vigorously into her coat. As he went from patch to patch, her coat first appeared moist, but it soon assumed a radiant shine. From the shape of the bottle I guessed the liquid was oil. I knew her coat was not infected, so the oil was being applied as a cosmetic. When the groom finished, the Queen of Suir stepped from the stall to the grooming mirror and peered proudly at herself. She appeared as if a young she hound in her prime.

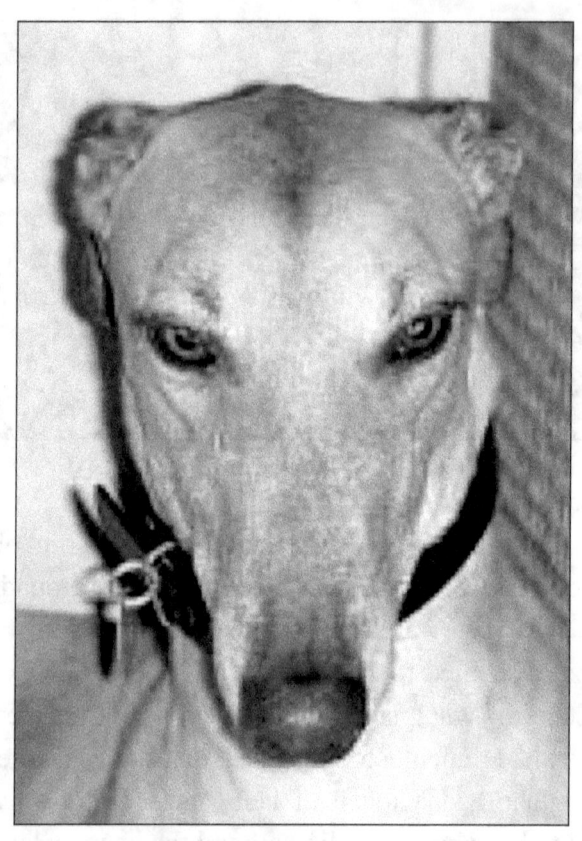

I had never before regarded her as old, but how could I have ever thought of her to be so young? Of course she had never appeared as young as Janice Lee, but neither had she ever looked as old as Colonel Flash. My surprise mounted as I watched her hesitate from the groom's urgings before returning to the stall. She was not really admiring herself for what she really was, but rather, with the oil, for what she appeared to be. When she finally returned to the stall, she did so as a different hound than when she had left it, for in the mirror she had seen the Lady Suir she had wanted to see, and now she seemed quite satisfied with what she saw. But I knew she had not seen herself in the mirror for what she was. She had seen an oiled image of her former self.

Why hadn't I ever seen her age before? Why hadn't I seen her clearly, for what she really was? Perhaps it was not because I couldn't see, but because I hadn't wanted to see. It then occurred to me that I had always used my eyes for seeing only what I wanted to see, not for what really was, and I suddenly wanted to see things as they were. I opened my eyes wide and scanned the grooming room, thinking as I did that for the first time in my life I was actually seeing what I was looking at.

The groom dug his thumb into my shoulder. I yelped and lurched sideways. I tried pulling away, but he held firmly onto my leg. My head began spinning with pain and I suddenly felt nauseous. Without further warning I spewed up a whole bellyful of foul stuff until every muscle in my body felt drained. I felt as though all the energy within me had just shot out of my mouth and spilled onto the cement floor around me.

The groom with the large hands held me upright as the other rushed off and returned shortly with a hose and washed the foul stuff down the drain in the stall. The scent almost made me upchuck again, but I was empty. The grooms soon returned to me, one brushing and one rubbing, but I could not get the smell out of my nose and, try as I did, I could not pretend as if the odour wasn't there.

Some time passed before old Flash trudged into the grooming room. An almost steady stream of perspiration poured from his heavy flanks and brisket. He passed by my stall, leaving a trail of wet paw prints behind, and my spirits soared. He lifted up his head as if to speak, but merely screwed up his nose, sniffed, then nodded brusquely as he passed by. The trainer led him to his stall where he collapsed with a sigh on his haunches and seemed oblivious to the frenzied activity of his grooms.

His appearance strengthened me. As the wretched taste left my mouth and my head cleared, uneasiness began stirring and growing inside me. I tried to pass it off—as if it were not there, but when it persisted, I couldn't help wondering what it was.

CHAPTER SEVEN

Ours was the seventh event of the day.

The bell, the thing whizzed by, the gate swung open. I started late, my timing was off, and I barely grabbed hold of fifth place out of the starting gate. The pack set a fast, demanding pace, but the crowd did not respond. The stadium seemed like a huge bowl filled with wet heat that stifled the pack as well as the people in the stadium. Only the thing we pursued looked untroubled by the sun's muggy heat.

Colonel Flash galloped triumphantly several lengths out front. For a moment I hardly recognized him. He had the speed of a young hound and an effortless style. His powerful gait was usually forced, but now his haunches rose and fell in a rapid, steady rhythm. His hind feet looked as though they were trying to overtake his forefeet. Even for a start, his pace was remarkable, and I guessed he would falter early—perhaps as early as the second turn.

Rainless the Red followed him by three lengths. No doubt he too was surprised by the Colonel's unusual burst of speed. Red's gallop was also unusually confident, but he seemed to have lost his composure, for now he was running as if unsure of himself.

Red and the Colonel were the only two of my close friends who ran in this event. Saint-Harry had been scheduled but got scratched at the last minute. Bonus and the Lady

Suir had run earlier chases. The two hounds in front and the one behind me were strangers.

The pack maintained its unusually fast pace despite the hot, wet air. We rounded the first quarter-turn without slackening our pace. The pack soon shot out of the second turn and rushed into the backstretch. The Colonel didn't drop back as I had expected, but with lagging energy I lapsed unchallenged into last place.

My body refused to yield itself to the chase. From time to time the nausea I had felt earlier returned, then quickly passed. My lungs absorbed the moist air and my breathing became heavier with every stride. My chest felt like a burden that I carried dangerously low to the ground. My left shoulder throbbed incessantly and I had no choice but to favor it so I ran slightly off balance. Sweat flowed freely from my forehead and seeped into my eyes, which burned and blurred my vision, but even blinking my eyes repeatedly didn't seem to help. Again and again, but each time in vain, I tried to concentrate on the bobbing ball of white puff that hopped up and down far out in front of the straining hounds.

The pack pulled slowly away from me. As the gap continued to widen, I wondered how the Colonel managed to hold his extraordinary pace—and on such a hot day. To expend oneself without reserve commanded my deepest respect. Like a fountain gone berserk, whole streams of sweat gushed wildly from the old Colonel's back. The entire pack was sprinkled by the Colonel's spewing perspiration as he thundered up ahead, proud leader of the chase. He drove on, appearing magnificent and invincible. He had totally committed himself to the task of chasing the thing *as if* it were a real hare, and *as if* some great truth lay beyond the chase itself. Perhaps the wisdom gleaned from experience and old age gave a hound enough faith and energy to chase an uncatchable thing around in a circle on such a day as today.

And so what about me? Why was I limping along, complaining and feeling sorry for myself? Was I just using the sun and my shoulder as excuses for not facing the way things were? I had kidded myself about the Queen of Suir, but then I was able to confront the truth of her appearance when she appeared before the mirror. Why not now as well? That the hare was a thing and that the chase was only a game did not stop the Colonel. He found meaning in the chase itself—in the act of chasing—without even hoping to catch the mechanical hare.

I looked again at the old hound. He hadn't slowed a bit. The sight of him running pell-mell at such a fast pace for so long inspired me. I suddenly felt ashamed of myself. And to think I had thought everything was senseless, without meaning! There was nothing senseless about the wild applause of the stadium crowds, or about the smell of the flowers and colorful ribbons in the Winner's Circle; about the evening talks with my fellow hounds, or sprinting alone in the meadow; or about the pleasures of Janice Lee who would one day whelp my pups and continue the ancient blood line of the Saluki pedigree. These things could continue to fulfill me as they had done so often in the past. Yes, to chase for the chase itself, and hoping, yes hoping and having faith that there is something beyond the chase and enjoying what is here and now for what it is, yes, of course, all this could

make me happy as it obviously has for the old Colonel.

My entire body awakened with these thoughts as I sucked in a large draught of air. Pushing down on my left forefoot, I felt that my shoulder was sound. I scoffed at myself: blaming the injury for my poor performance had merely been an excuse. I had imagined most of the heat today and my fatigue was only between my ears!

Surveying the pack I saw their positions had not changed. Rainless the Red had gained a trifle on the Colonel, but the old hound continued to hold his lead with spirit and stamina—a remarkable feat.

I hurled myself forward as we sped around the third quarter-turn. I shot quickly past the three hounds unknown to me who, from sheer astonishment, dropped even further behind. I crept up cautiously behind Red knowing I could easily overtake him, but the move needed strategy.

The crowd began roaring and broadcast my charge, so

having no time for tactics, I propelled forward along the inside rail. Now alerted to my approach, Red glanced around to see me coming up fast on his left flank. As if to make way, he drifted slyly toward the adjoining right lane, but then he lowered his head and bolted across to block me.

I changed my pace, feinted toward him, and suddenly drew back.

Thrown off balance, with surprise frozen on his face, Red flashed across in front of me and slammed bluntly into the rail.

I rushed by him but slowed as I advanced behind Colonel Flash. He had not noticed neither my rally nor Red's attempt to block it. I decided not to challenge or overtake him if he maintained his pace. That he had not yet lost his steam both baffled and pleased me.

Mount Hoop rose in sight and appeared strangely unreal behind the heat waves that appeared to ripple in the still afternoon air, but without even a trace of wind. Such still-ness was uncommon for the track, especially at this time of day. The summer usually brought its thick humidity, but almost always the wind kept it moving. The insistent sun blared down without the shade of a single cloud and with such intensity that even the bleached white marble of the bas-relief appeared to be scorching hot.

The Colonel was making a peculiar effort. Although he always ran hard and gave it his all, I had never seen him gallop as strongly as today. I wondered if the old hound was running his heart out just to prove to me that chasing *as if* the hare were real could be done. But if that were so, why was proving that to me so important to him?

Then, just as we swung out of the third turn and neared the bas-relief, the Colonel broke stride and slowed.

I fell back, alarmed.

Colonel Flash wavered unsteadily for several paces and then, as if catching a second wind, he caught hold of himself and slowly regained his lost strides.

I doubted that he could maintain his now faltering pace until he reached the finish line. But to peter out at the last corner of such a memorable chase would be truly heart breaking for the old hound. No one had ever better deserved the laurels of the winner's Circle. I longed to do something for him, as he had done for me, but I was helpless. The cruelty of an old hound's aging limbs knew no bounds and gave no mercy. He must do it himself or not at all. Within the grips of the chase, the chase gripped each hound alone.

But perhaps there was another way. He didn't know I was right behind him and running only because of his kind counsel last night. If he realized that his words had inspired me, perhaps seeing me chasing today and right behind him might inspire him. If I could move up alongside him so he could see me, then fall back and follow him in to the finish line…

Colonel Flash thundered close along the rail and the whole track seemed to quake under his weight. As I advanced and drew abreast, his astonished head snapped my way. His eyes rolled, he gasped loudly and fell back.

I slowed with him, hoping he would see what I was trying to do. But Red seized the chance to pass us easily on the outside. The other hounds moved up close behind.

Galloping side by side, I urged the Colonel on. Again his

eyes rolled strangely and his face was twisted. Our pace slowed even more and another hound passed us by.

I motioned him forward by nodding my head. He didn't respond. I shouted that he was too close to quit now—just one more turn, the homestretch, then the kennels. But he didn't seem to hear me. I tried to think of something else to do or say. Just then he caught up with himself and bolted forward for what I hoped would be his rally to the finish line.

Instead the Colonel shuddered violently and his entire body heaved sideways. The two hounds that were running behind us dashed quickly by. The crowd's shouting increased and became a sustained roar that seemed to join forces with the sun and beat without mercy down upon me.

The Colonel lost control of his legs. He swayed unsteadily and then began groping across the lanes toward the bas-relief. But before reaching the outside lane, his forelegs buckled beneath him, his chin dug into the ground and, coming to a sliding stop, as if propped up by something underneath, his hindquarters remained upright. For a moment he looked as if he had found and was uprooting a mole hole. Then a great sigh issued from his lungs, he shuddered and fell heavily on his side, spent. His heart had burst.

I stood as if rooted like a tree to the track. The sun caressed the waves of pulsing moisture that seeped from my brow. The stadium flag high atop the pole rippled once, then stopped. The scene burned itself deeply into my mind: The Colonel lay without life facing the bas-relief, but the monument stood in silence far from his reach. The spectre kept burning in my eyes until I began to see things as they were, and until I slowly realized that the hare's absence from the marble scene of chasing hounds was as ludicrous as the absence of breath from the Colonel's steaming body.

I was only vaguely aware of being lifted, placed feet first in a kennel cart, and wheeled quickly off the track.

CHAPTER EIGHT

I lay on my mat, dreaming:

Running fast, without thought. Like an outstretched foreleg, a bamboo pole extends from beneath my shoulder, where it is strapped to my belly by the tight jacket girth. The tip of the pole is so far in the distance it is hardly visible and the sunset glints from its slick surface. But it is pointed toward the heart of Hoop Mountain and the lance leads the way, so I follow without a second thought.

A vast, grassless plain carpets out before me. I am separated only by distance from Hoop's unsuspecting heart. My paws sometime sink pleasantly into the soft mounds that rise from fresh rodent holes, but my steady gallop is otherwise undisturbed. As I advance, the wind grows silent but a flock of large jackdaws circling above caw relentlessly. I yawn and scan the empty landscape for a tree of shade, but seeing nothing but dry grasses, I run on, onward.

The jackdaws suddenly flutter skyward and vanish into a violet cloud. I look up and then understand. A grey falcon, their hungry prey and scout of the mountain, hovers high overhead. Its eyes pierce mine menacingly and I must look away. The violet cloud then darkens ominously until it bursts and spews down a torrent of rain. The quickly muddied soil under my feet tugs at my pasterns. At first puddles form in the field but soon merge to become pools and then a shallow pond, but as if by magic my bamboo pole transforms into a flat board that I use to paddle my way from the muddy pond to dry ground. The falcon soars off to warn the mountain I am coming.

Forewarned, sly Hoop soon makes rise a forest before me. Joined branch to branch and root to root, the community of trees sways and groans in unison. My paddle that was once a pole becomes a rope as I approach the swooning forest at full gallop. Weaving itself cleverly through the entanglements, the rope pulls me through the menacing forest as simply as a beetle on a string. I am pulled through the twisted trees and amused by the futile efforts of the swatting branches and grasping roots. I emerge from the menace unharmed and alone, standing on the foothill of the mountain.

But before I can ready myself for the charge, a river splashes across my path. It sweeps past me flowing from the heights of the mountain and begins to circle and form a moat around the base of old Hoop. Boulders spill out from the banks and, tumbling across the current, they form a touchstone footbridge for boatless travelers. Grateful, I hop on top of a rock, which rolls to throw me from its back, but not before I leap onto the next, jumping from one rock to another, zigzagging across the river until mid-stream, then the boulders turn into tree trunks, rising at once from the river floor, then begin floating slowly downstream. I turn to retrace my steps, but already the stones behind are wooden logs bobbing on the water and bumping into one another. The rock I am standing on begins to tremble.

My pole begins to probe for the river's bottom in search of seating. Soon it finds firm ground. Then, vaulting high and dry above the water's splashing jaws, my paws plunk firmly down on the mountain's unprotected belly.

The vaulting pole becomes a lance and I seat its stock against my shoulder. Now only a short distance lay between me and Hoop Mountain's vital organ and, now braced for the impact, I lower my head and gallop forward.

As the lance point touches the mountain's breast, an enormous cavern suddenly yawns open, and the lock-jawed hole consumes me. Without breaking stride, I plunge headlong into Hoop's dark confines. The light diminishes as behind me the opening slowly closes. I stumble forward without sight, bounding against one shadow only to rebound from the nest. Pinnacles of cold silence hang downward from the cave and jut upward from the floor. Echoes fade into the darkness like cloud tufts in the night.

I stumble forward, though I might be running backwards or in circles. Up ahead I spy daylight squeezing through a crack in the solid stone. The sliver widens into a crack as I run toward it; then, like a wedge, the light pries open a slit in the rock and the gap expands until full daylight rushes in. I burst outside as the tunnel exit closes, but I stop at once.

I stand teetered on the narrow ledge of some overhanging place. Stumped, I peer across at the infinite distance to the opposite side and look down into the infinite depth of a ravine. I hear the mountain disappearing behind me; I watch across the way to see it reappear as a vague and complacent cloud. I calmly turn my lance into a vaulting pole, but it cannot reach the bottom of the floorless depression. In a sudden dash of rage, I coil the pole into a rope and cast it toward the other side. It falls short and I watch with dread as it descends to vanish forever from my sight. I wheel around but see only the open plain that I know will never again lure me into it. I turn with resolution to face my world's abyss…

Something tugged hesitantly on my paw. I tried opening my eyes, feeling grateful to be freed from the world of dreams, but its strange embrace held me and my eyes refused to obey me and open. It was as if I had no will, no power to command even my own body. Yet, in my mind's eye, the inner room of my coop was oddly vivid in its smallest detail. I envisioned it all without opening my eyes.

Above me spanned a flat roof and around me rose four safe walls, from one of which hung a swinging door that opened into the outer, open-air room. Inside, the cracked floor was clutter with my mood. Tufts of hair and dried morsels of meat were strewn everywhere except for the area beneath my mat. An untouched plate of food and a half-filled water bowl lay in one corner; propped against another corner and tilted at a slight angle, with its rotted and untasted meat hanging in strips, stood the Colonel's T-bone. In the third corner across from my mat lay a mound of dung that had accumulated since my confinement and life of dreams. The outer room was enclosed by a wire mesh screen and had a natural earthen floor but no ceiling. An artificial tree trunk was planted near the center of the room. An exercise stump, the driftwood piece was twisted into a graceful shape, a bird in flight. In a corner lay a badly chewed rubber ball and, from the wire mesh screen, hung the thick gnawing rope I once used to clean my teeth.

Again, someone nudged me.

My eyes pulled regretfully open. Saint-Harry stood over

me breathing intently through stern nostrils. My coop was obscured in the night's sightless eyes; darkness glared from every direction and I wondered if I had really awakened or was still dreaming.

Where's the sun? I asked.

Harry replied that it had been down now for some time.

Groggy and with a dry and rank mouth, I rose and pulled myself to the water bowl. I brushed past Saint-Harry and a volley of electric sparks crackled between our shorthair coats. My senses sharpened a trifle. The water I drank looked stale, but I could not taste my suspicion. I recalled that since I had nipped Old Smokey in the heel last week, he had stopped tending to my coop.

Saint-Harry was anxious. He said he wanted to talk, that something important had risen, that as much as he disliked it, he had been delegated by the other hounds to speak with me.

I swung open the door and peered outside. The night had fallen but as yet the moon had not appeared overhead. I would soon be dashing into the field and running until I was spent, then return to my coop to sleep, to dream, to forget as I had been doing of late but did not know for how long.

As I thought about the field and the pleasure of sheer exhaustion I felt after running freely in it, suddenly I remembered the break in the fence I had discovered last week. It lay in an area beyond the Sea Foam stone on the far side of the knoll. An old tree had fallen in a thunderstorm. The fence had been repaired, but in haste and poorly. A hole large enough for a hound remained between the patched areas. Lately that hole had come to possess me, but in its vacancy I seemed to be powerless. I could neither erase it from my mind nor bring myself to slip though it. The opening in the fencing taunted me like an open mouth, its parted lips mocking my indecision. It seemed absurd to remain in the kennels where I could no longer find satisfaction in the chase. I slept and ran in order to tire and sleep again. Escape to freedom in the world outside the kennels would be simple enough if I acted before the fence was properly fixed, but something prevented me from leaving.

That the hare was a thing was the only certainty I now possessed. The Colonel's powerful faith had burst his heart —for what? It was unimportant whether or not there was something beyond the chase, or that the chase meant something that I could not understand. To live only for what might be was living in wait for something that might never come. No, in order to be made happy by chasing, a hound must believe that the chase had some meaning. But how could the chase have meaning if the hare the hounds were chasing simply was not a real creature but a mechanical thing? Impossible. And to be happy chasing as if the hare were real was equally as impossible. Of what value was the night if a hound spent his days running in circles chasing something that was nothing? To live only to watch one day sneak up behind you and pass senselessly into the next day was intolerable. Each day the Lady Sur wrinkled a little more and slowly withered into an ugly hound; the Colonel galloped in hundreds of chases in as many years simply to bury his proud nose into the very track he ran on. So what was the use of it all? Old hounds live only to grow older in order to die? From the starting trap to the finish line: to simply put in one's time? Was that what it was all about? If so, that life was all about

nothing. If so, why should he be duped into playing a game that had no pleasure, no prize, no winner? Why, as Lady Suir, play tricks on your eyes with a mirror? And why, like my brooding self, did I stay in the kennels simply to die. With what is known right here and the great unknown lying outside, why couldn't I push myself through that broken fence and flee to freedom?

Forward Cheque! Harry commanded.

I turned resolutely from the door. His presence annoyed me.

Don't you hear me? Do you think I am talking to myself?

I shrugged and turned again to peer outside.

But Harry was insistent.

I don't know what has come over you since the Colonel collapsed, but your brooding has gone on far too long. The moon has changed from half to full. You are not doing yourself any good and the entire kennel is worried about you.

My tail began swinging impatiently.

You have turned away from the entire kennel and now they are beginning to turn from you. You enraged Red by accusing him of your accident when immediately after it you had blamed only yourself. Bonus won't have anything to do with you since you called him a lowbred mutt. Janice Lee is in tears most of the time. You insult the Queen of Suir by avoiding her —her, of all hounds! And since you nipped Old Smokey in the ankle, he's become afraid of all of us and now neglects our coops. And, I might add, you have offended me by keeping to yourself when, at one time anyway, we were the closest of friends. But right now that is not important. Besides, I've gotten used to your indifference.

Harry tired me. My thoughts kept wandering to the field where I'd soon be running.

But Harry continued. You know you were disgraced when carted off the track when the Colonel died. In fact, you brought disgrace on all of us. The other hounds were ready then to run you out of the kennels. But I stuck by you and told them how much the Colonel had meant to you. They accepted that for a few days, but they started up again when you didn't begin chasing right away. So I began defending you with your injured shoulder. But that didn't work at all, especially after you stopping limping and began tromping through the field all night. Right now they're in the yard howling up another storm. So, tell me, Forward Cheque, just how will I defend your strangeness now?

Defend me, I exploded, you won't! I don't need defending and you don't need a reason. I don't care what they think of me, not anymore, and that goes the same for you if you think you must defend me to yourself. But don't misunder-stand me. It's nothing you or the others did or did not do. It's just that I don't care any longer. Now I'm tired of talking. Nothing can come of it. I'm going for a jaunt.

Looking stern, Harry said he wasn't through.

I'll be frank, he said brusquely. I don't think I want to defend you now—even if I could, no, not anymore. But that isn't why I've come. Something far more serious has arisen. I'm not here tonight as a friend, but as a speaker for the entire kennel.

Harry's voice tightened and I began to listen more closely.

He continued soberly: the Colonel's death and your injured shoulder don't explain your strange behavior. We know it's got to be something else. We keep recalling the day of the bumping bout accident and your fantasy story about catching the hare. At the time we all thought you were either joking or trying to avoid embarrassment for falling in the chase. We had almost forgotten all about it. But the more estranged you become, the more we recall and talk about your tale. We know what you said was not believable, but now we can't get it out of our minds. It's most likely false, we all know that, but then there is a remote chance it might be true. The problem is that we don't know for sure, and that very doubt has crept into our minds. It is as contagious as the mange and has infected the entire kennel. We've tried to forget it, but then it itches all the more. We've tried ignoring it, and for a time it seems to disappear, but then it crops up again worse than ever. We've scratched and clawed ourselves raw just talking about it, but the itching simply won't stop and now we're all tired of the open sores.

In short, he continued, we want an explanation. You've become a wretched hound, insensitive and strange. Your coop reeks so badly that we've come to walking around it. And your unkempt coat smells worse. You sleep all day and run wild in the field all night. And now it's time you must tell us why.

Speaking so low that Harry had to strain forward to hear me, I replied that what troubled me, troubled me alone. It involved neither him nor the rest of the hounds in the kennel. I told him not to pry and not to be concerned. I then asked him to leave because the moon had risen and I wanted to take a sprint.

I turned and strode out the door, but stopped short. A dozen or so hounds had gathered outside. Several others were coming through the shadows toward my coop. Saint-Harry tugged at my tail and I went back inside.

This has troubled us more than you thought, he said. You see, if your tale of the hare is true, then you are distraught for good reason and the rest of us are chasing something unreal and our lives are a lie. On the other hand, if your tale is false, then you are suffering from distemper, in which case you are the potential cause of a life-threatening epidemic. So, either way, Forward Cheque, you are causing us harm, untold harm. And although we are mortified by the possibility of chasing a false hare and terrified of dying of distemper, our greatest dread comes from the doubt, from not knowing which to believe. We're tired of this irritation that won't go away. We want our peace of mind back. We must know the truth—at any cost.

As Harry spoke, I realized that although he was asking for truth, it was certainty, a peace of mind—not the truth—that he was actually seeking. That the chase was a hoax was true, but it was also true that everything else was uncertain. So If I told them the truth, I would be giving them true doubt. And doubt is what they do not want. They want me to be their kennel surgeon and tell them they don't have the mange; that if the truth itches, don't scratch, or else the itch will become a mange of doubt. Instead they should pretend their itch was from a passing flea or mite, an errant idea of the mind. Yes, that's what they want to hear.

A hound barked outside.

Well? Harry insisted

I knew before I spoke that I'd decided to be their calming kennel surgeon. I told Harry that he'd always been a loyal friend, and that I realized I had treated him poorly of late, but that something had happened that made me different from him.

The truth about the hare! He demanded.

Slowly, so my lie would be convincing, I said the story had been false. As far as I knew the hare was a real creature, not a thing as I had said. I apologized for making him and the other hounds think otherwise.

Harry did not look convinced. He stood in a proud, show hound stance with his legs slightly parted and his lean jaw raised stubbornly. His strong gaze discomforted me, and I wondered if perhaps he really did want the truth after all, and if the lie I had just told him would only increase his doubts.

The hounds outside began barking impatiently, causing quite a ruckus.

Forward Cheque, Harry said grimly, I don't—I can't believe you. I know you better than the others do. I listened more carefully to your story that night and, during the past two weeks, I've watched you closer than anyone else. You must tell me the truth. If not for the other's sake, at least for mine. Your story turns over and over in my mind. I can't get rid of it. One suspicion raises ten more. And the constant wondering and never knowing is driving me mad…

I had never seen Harry so possessed.

He said brokenly that he had even begun dreaming about my encounter with the hare.

I wondered why the truth should be dreaded so. Why should the truth about the false hare give a hound the invisible mange of doubt? If such a disease exists, why try to avoid it? Why pretend it isn't there and hope for something else? If the facts were faced, if the infection were accepted for the condition it is, why wouldn't the irritation cease to exist?

Red poked his head into the door of my coop.

He asked Harry what was taking so long.

Without removing his eyes from mine, Saint-Harry replied that he would be out in a minute.

Red huffed and withdrew.

Well? Harry asked.

I asked how he would know even if I told him the truth.

Harry thought for a moment, then sighed and said I was the only source they had. They no longer had the Colonel who could advise them about such things. Besides, he concluded, after everything he had told me, he didn't think I could lie to him any longer.

I nodded, agreeing with his logic, and went over to where he stood. I told him that I would give him the truth if he wanted it, but he must promise to do with it exactly what I asked. I added that it might be harmful to the others because they would not be able to understand it as easily as Harry would.

His ears arched suspiciously, but he agreed.

I admitted that the tale about the hare was true. What we believed to be a hare was actually a thing—but wait—he should not jump to conclusions. The Colonel also knew this to be true, which is why he had gotten upset that night I told the others. He had warned that the truth could drive the hounds to despair, then madness. But the Colonel had a deeper thought. He said it wasn't important for the hare to be a real creature. He believed that a hound should chase as if the thing on the track were real…as if there was something to it we could not see or understand, that we had to chase the thing on faith that there was more.

Harry looked stunned.

I continued, asking Harry to think about the bas-relief in which the hounds were immortalized in marble while chasing the hare, but the hare portion of the carving that had been broken off was symbolic of our condition. Aren't the hounds running as if the hare were still there?

Outside a pair of hounds growled and snapped at each other.

Harry looked dazed.

I explained that I had told him the truth because it would be easier for him to live with the Colonel's thought rather than with the mange-like doubt of not knowing about the hare. But that didn't hold for the other hounds because they would either think Harry was now mad or the truth itself would do them terrible harm.

A lone hound wailed just outside the door of the coop. It sounded like the Lady Suir.

Harry stood in a stupor, motionless.

So this is what you must do, I continued. Tell the others that my story about the false hare was not true because... well, say because I had made a bad showing that day and, hoping to regain the respect I thought I had lost, I'd hobbled in on an injured foot and told them a windy tale so I wouldn't look so bad to them. Yes, and explain to them my recent estrangement as a result of my guilt and shame for not telling them the truth about my poor showing. When the Colonel unveiled my tale before them as false, I thought I had lost my reputation. You can also tell them I was ashamed for being wheeled off the track when the Colonel died. Tell them these things, Harry, and their mange will be cured, their doubts dispelled. As I finished I felt relieved, yet strangely fearful.

Harry seemed to have understood and believed me.

Bonus called into the coop and asked if Harry needed any help.

What about the Colonel's death, then, Harry asked.

What did he mean?

The way the colonel...passed on.

Natural, Harry, he died a natural death. He ran his last race as his best race and his heart burst.

And you believe in the Colonel's way?

Of course, I answered, feigning conviction.

Then why aren't you running in the chase?

Harry had trapped me. He'd sensed that I had told him only part of the truth. I had to act quickly to avoid destroying everything I had tried to do to restore his peace of mind.

I told him that, actually, I had been planning to run in tomorrow's chase; that it had taken me a long time to sort things out and to understand the meaning of what the Colonel had shared with me.

Saint-Harry looked unconvinced and stood silent for a while. Then he seemed to grasp hold of something, nodded distractedly, and went outside to join the other hounds. They quieted down as he began talking. I heard only an occasional word, but he continued, his voice became more animated until a weird, high-pitched laughter burst from his throat and rang out in the still night. The others began yapping excitedly and, like young pups, headed playfully toward the exercise yard. While leaving, as a token of their understanding and forgiveness, one by one each hound raised his leg and left a few friendly drops of water on the side of my coop.

Contempt for them and self-disgust turned over like worms in my belly. I threw myself against the wall. Falling backwards, I began clawing savagely at the mat. It shredded easily and cotton stuffing flew everywhere. I covered myself with the debris and then sought desperately for the solace of sleep. But the harder I tried, the more impossible it was to forget myself. I began rolling around on the floor and upset the water bowl, splashing cold liquid on the dirt floor and matting my coat with mud. Then I struck the colonel's T-bone in the corner. I clenched it between my jaws, tasted the foul and rotten meat, and then spat it from my mouth. I lay staring at the black strips of dried flesh hanging from the white bone. Enraged with fear, I snatched it up and fled from the coop.

Running swiftly through the kennels, I bounded into the open field and headed for the broken fence beyond the stone of Sea Foam. The bone in my mouth blocked the easy flow of air but the difficulty seemed to urge me faster on. I glanced briefly over my shoulder. The stadium rose out of the valley like a silent, foreboding growth, and several faintly glowing lights dotted the kennel area. The scene was washed with a light but steady glow from the moon.

The kennel world offered me everything and gave me nothing. It teased me with impossible lies. The Colonel teased me with another. Yes, with what food am I left if I refuse to eat their bones? If I starve myself I'll see only a shadow when I stand before the grooming mirror. I'll be less

than the reflected image of a cloud lazing across the surface of a pond. If I deny the food, the food denies me.

I ask the hare in my head, what's it all about?

The head hare leers, saying I've no choice but to chase him, the mirror image of myself.

No! I counter: I have a choice!

Unruffled, the head-hare continued: Although it means nothing if you chase me, you mean nothing if you don't. I am either wood chips in your mouth or you are haze before a mirror. Which is better, hound: to be a rotter, keeping only to yourself, living only for yourself, meaning nothing even to yourself? Or to be a plugger, like the Colonel, hoping there is something else, living each day as it passes into night—as if it were something more than another day?

I answered to the hare in my head: Hare, if you were real, you would feel my teeth, and I'd crush you like a fishbone. But you're not real, your something made of air, and my jaws need something solid to chew on. There's food outside that fence, there's freedom, too, and that's the choice I have.

Midway through the field, I ran off the well-trod path and began jumping through the short grasses. The brittle grain stalks snapped off and pricked my underbelly. At first the pesky tingles annoyed me, but my belly was soon full with a herd of nipping, gnawing vermin. For a time I felt freed from the hunger of myself. When feeding time came again, I would be devouring the fresh meat of freedom far beyond the fence.

A thick vine snagged my forepaw. I stumbled and stopped at once. I had wandered into a perilous area of briar plants. I scanned the field around me, but the grass was too tall to see anything. The danger lay all around me, waiting with the patience known only by a trap. Upon realizing the menacing briars surrounded me, I became strangely exalted but also tense and very alert. I planned an evasive course for my escape, cocked myself into a hurling crouch, then sprang into the air and began running pell-mell toward the general direction of the broken fence. A briar scratched my ear and dragged along my left side. I darted off toward the right. Feeling that I was both chasing and being chased, I wondered if I was the briar's quarry or its hound. Either way, this chase was at least a real one. I outwitted the barbed thing— or it outwitted me—for another twenty years.

Then a coiled vine snared my hock and pulled me down. I lay motionless for a time, regained my wind, then retrieved the Colonel's T-bone and was off again. A dozen steps further I sprawled headlong into an ensnarling briar plant. I tried wrenching myself free, yowling as countless thorns pricked and tore my skin, but the forest of gnarly vines only held me tighter. The more I struggled, the more entwined and entrapped I became. Then I lay still, to catch my breath, to think.

The trap enraged me but the pain I felt from the barbs was curiously inspiring. Slowly, I urged myself on. My back legs caught hold of something solid. It felt like a crooked root that had raised itself from beneath the field for this very purpose. I hooked my ankles beneath it and inched slowly backwards. My impulse was to stand upright and wrest myself loose from the twisted maze. But I held back and finally pulled myself free.

In a near frenzy I ran diagonally across the field until once again I found the path. I veered onto the well-worn sod, felt the smooth soil beneath my paws, and stayed on the trail. I sweated freely, despite the chilled night air. The salty moisture that came from my skin began tormenting the bleeding scratches beneath my coat. The rage of pain soon mellowed to a throbbing anger and spurred me forward to my freedom at the broken fence.

Ascending to the knoll's peak with ease, I slowed upon approaching the Sea Foam stone. Cocking my head, I flung the Colonel's T-bone with all my strength; I heard it strike the rock's surface, then fall resolutely to the ground. The sound stopped me. I returned to where the bone had fallen, then dug a deep hole at the base of the stone and buried the wretched thing. I anointed the grave with all the water that was inside me.

I strode more easily through the pine trees, down the back slope, and pulled up before the high fence. All I needed

was to hurl myself safely through the jagged wire that fringed the gaping hole and catch myself on the other side. Over there, freedom had no bounds. The food was there. I had only to seek it out, then feast. And I could go anywhere—and for any reason, instead of chasing around in circles after a thing we had been told was a creature. Beyond the fence there would be no tight jacket cinched around my girth, no herd of hounds to hem me in, no starting trap or finish line. No chasing circles out there. Beyond the fence is a new world, a whole world.

I stopped and stood before the fence, peering through the hole.

One short leap through the opening would free me from the senseless kennel world. Well? Well, how could I be sure this is what I really wanted? How does a hound ever know what he wants—especially when his choice would be for all time?

I felt as though I could have or do anything I wanted, if only I wanted something badly enough to have. But did I really want to flee? Flight for what…to what? And freedom? Freedom from what? Freedom to what? What lurked out there in that darkness besides dangers and death? It couldn't be less and it might be more, but what if outside was the same as inside the fence? And what if chasing and not chasing the hare meant exactly the same thing? Wasn't the world out there just as uncertain as the one inside the kennel—and maybe even more so?

Besides, either inside or outside the fence, of what am I really certain? I am certain the Lady Suir wrinkles more each day, that the Colonel is dead, and that the hare and the chase are without sense. Of everything else, I am uncertain. These are the only morsels in my teeth. All the rest are merely smells in my nose.

So what about the fence? Inside it I will either collapse on the track while chasing a shadow or rot in my coop like a sack of old meat. And outside the fence is a world of unknowns. If there was no reason to stay, it might follow that there was no reason not to stay. Am I to sit here by the fence chewing up and eating myself when I'm actually only starving myself? Where is the food of myself hidden? Does the answer lie somewhere within me, far down inside, or is the bottom deeper than my underbelly? Can a mouth have a belly whose food is itself? Should I go forward, backwards or sit here forever and devour myself with questions answered by questions that have no answers?

Confused beyond repair and overwhelmed with shame, I turned my back on the fence.

As I jogged back to the kennels, a welcomed ache crept into my limbs and back. At least the fatigue would bring me relief until I awoke. I began thinking of sleep. My thoughts drained through me like a drug and I yearned to fall into the stupor of my mat. As my passing for sleep increased, so increased the strength in my legs. I fairly flew over the knoll's hump, past the Sea Foam stone, and down the inclined field to the kennels.

CHAPTER NINE

Several paces from my coop I was clobbered by the pungent odor of a she hound in heat. Coming from the fresh air of the fields, the thick scent staggered and nearly overwhelmed me. A nausea similar to that I had felt in the grooming room surged within me. I knew Janice Lee was waiting for me inside my coop. The scene I imagined with her was intolerable. So, skirting quietly around the coop, I concealed myself in the shadows some distance beyond. I knew she would soon become discouraged and leave.

I stood waiting in the shadows and thought of how tired of her I had become, of how senseless it was to waste away inside some she hound. She, like all the others, lived a simple, easygoing life. She felt that only the unborn pups directed the affairs of hounds. Without one unpleasant thought between her ears, she got all her pleasure from between her legs. To her, the chase simply was what it was. She understood nothing of my problems—and, she didn't even know she didn't understand. Such bliss was no longer a part of me and I was no longer a part of her world. Lately, she had left my coop dragging her sadness behind her. I had jumped on and off her quickly, then sent her on her way. The more she wanted, the less I seemed capable of giving, and whatever it was I needed, she did not have. She always pleaded for something more, as if some wondrous meaning lay beyond the act itself. Tonight I did not feel any desire for even fast relief. In fact, the more I thought of mating her, the more repulsed I became. It was just as absurd to sink one's life into a she hound as it was to burn it out in the chase.

I heard some sounds approaching behind me. The evening talks were breaking up. The hounds were yapping excitedly about something, but only a few words were distinct…Saint-Harry…odd…a wild pup…unlike the hound. They saw me standing in the shadows outside my coop, hesitated for a minute, then awkwardly bade me the night and hurried past me to their own coops. But when some distance away, no doubt thinking I was beyond earshot, they yipped and snickered. Their laughter struck me with the force of the trainer's crop. It was obvious: they couldn't help but smell Janice Lee and had drawn their own conclusions about why I was standing alone in the shadows outside my coop.

Why was I standing there like a mutt gone mad? Simply to avoid confronting the panting hound inside? Why didn't I face up and tell her that she no longer did to me what needed to be done, whatever that was. Why couldn't I just tell her that I could no longer tolerate her presence, that I wanted to be rid of her, that I simply wanted to nip it off between us? Was it because I didn't know what I wanted and therefore could not choose what I did not want?

Anger drove me into my coop.

My sudden entrance startled her. She jumped up from the mat. No doubt she had been snoozing, for her eyes looked glazed. She was a headful of simple, sleepy dreams. Hesitating for a moment, she then bounded to me and lapped affectionately at my muzzle.

She had been eating fishmeal.

I ducked under her wet tongue and strode briskly to the mat where I threw myself down. Her neck drooped and she sank to her haunches in the center of the coop. My repulsion rose like a phlegm in my throat, then dried into a hard knot of fear. I wanted to end it quickly, or at least I thought I did, but could I do it? Would she become another hole in the fence for me? No! I mustered myself.

Speaking sternly, I told her that I no longer felt for her and that I could not continue to pretend otherwise.

Her head jerked in disbelief.

It isn't that I can't mate you—it's that I don't want to mate you.

Her eyes were baffled with moisture.

I explained that the exact reason was complicated but she could be assured it was not anything she had or had not done. She looked as if I had chomped her on the snout. I went further, saying that I now chased a quarry quite different than the track hare; that I now ran in a different chase, one that had no track or starting gate or finish line; that the event was without spectators and, finally, that I was the only hound running. In short, I finished; I am alone, absolutely alone in a chase of my own.

A long silence separated us further.

She finally said she thought she understood.

And, for an instant, I really thought she had.

Then she rose and came to me. She said if that was what I wanted, that there was nothing she could do.

An immense burden seemed to lift from me, and I felt both relieved and tired. I was groggy, much groggier than

85

before, and I yearned for the peace of the mat beneath me.

She said she had sensed something wrong since my accident; that I had become a stranger to her as well as to the other hounds.

Impatience began to gnaw at me.

She said I would probably think this a little odd, she did so herself, but I would make her very happy if I mated her tonight, just one more time.

I turned away, disgusted. She hadn't understood a thing. I had howled down from my mountain and, from her valley far below, she had not heard a sound. Either her deafness or my faint voice confirmed the distance between us. It made me feel even more alone than when I had lost the friendship of Lady Suir.

She pleaded that she would never trouble me again. But tonight, for some reason, it was important to her.

I looked at her squarely. My impulse was to run her out

that very instant. But then I asked myself what difference made one more night if afterwards I would be rid of her forever? And then it occurred to me that, once again, I had no clear-cut reaction. I had no definite answer to her definite question; I could either take her or throw her out. As with the fence, the choice was pressing but utterly impossible to make.

Janice Lee interpreted my silence as consent. The odour thickened as she neared me. I lay impassive a she nibbled questionably at my paw. But even my indifference seemed to urge her on. She became bolder and muzzled against my loins. My insides tumbled sickly. Her tongue shot into my underbelly. I lay without responding and felt as though I had no more relation to her yearning that a bowl of water had to a thirsty hound. Why did I allow myself to be handled like some kind of a thing? To be a tool to tinker with? To subject myself with neither will nor want to lie beneath the flanks of some hot she hound? She became stronger as a beast of sense and I became the weaker object of her demanding want. Was this what I had come to?

I snarled and bolted upright, hot with anger.

Terror flew from her eyes and she cowered from me.

Her fear and my awakened power raised me keenly alert. Proudly and with defiance I towered before her, glaring with such a wild and scornful intensity that sheer horror overcame her desire. She began to quiver, then stood shaking with fear under my assertion. I waited until she had lost nearly all control over her trembling limbs. I then stepped slowly toward her and she shrank backwards, fearful of my curled flews. Her mounting fear somehow heightened and enraged my own desire. She backed up nearly to the door.

Then I took her.

She mated fiercely, as a single organ of her senses, while I—strangely distant from it all—took exquisite pleasure in her antics and felt nothing but disgust.

I knew then I had completely lost the pleasure of a she hound. After that, what remained? Lately I hadn't enjoyed her as much as I had in the past, but never before had I been unable to lose and forget myself within her. Yet, as I looked back, except for sleeping, nothing had really satisfied me since the Colonel's death, no, since the encounter with the thing and discovering the hare was a hoax.

Everything I sensed seemed either numb, bland or grey. Fresh smells were vague memories of the past. All food tasted like so much mash; the sun's incessant rise and fall was fitfully dull; chatting with Harry or the others was a tedious and wasted task, and even running in the field was not for pleasure but fatigue. Everything I perceived became monotonous, and I had become monotony's humdrum hound.

I looked at Janice Lee. She could be fulfilled by the passion of a passing moment. Her submission was complete: she was totally absorbed and oblivious to everything except her senses.

What was I doing?

Mating Janice Lee was nothing less than giving into another illusion in a mirror, another game. We are simply playing who is the stronger of the two, a she hound or a he hound. I had moved from the track where I chased one thing to my coop where I mated another. Only the setting was different. If I couldn't chase as if it meant something, how can

I possibly mate as if I felt something?

I backed away from her and wilted in impotent rage.

She turned wonderingly.

Out! I barked!

She stood paralyzed in disbelief.

Out of my coop!

She howled and scurried out the door.

I jumped from the mat and hunched in vain over the dung pile in the corner. I began munching on some pellets of meal, then spat them on the floor and strode to the out room of my coop. A faint moonlight shone forebodingly on the twisted piece of driftwood.

Back inside, I flopped down on the mat, then yelped as my tail crinkled beneath me. I sprang up, enraged at the throbbing thing. I waved it around to stop the pain, but accidently smacked it against the wall. I began whipping it rashly around and, with open jaws, I grabbed for but missed it. I kept flailing it back and forth, then lunged and grasped it firmly between my teeth. I rocked my head gently up and down to soothe my broken tail. But the pain only increased, so I swabbed it with my tongue and tasted where my teeth had broken the skin. Then it slipped from my mouth and swung around behind me. The pain continued, so I bent myself almost double and moved my rump until the tail was swinging to and fro; then, stepping forward, I clamped it in my jaws and began following it around. My tail evaded me, or rather pulled itself into myself, so I walked faster to keep it from getting away. My hind end was pulling the tail from my jaws and my front end pushed forward to keep up. My feet obeyed themselves and began following one another. Then my feet broke from a walk into a lope, then began tramped into a four-legged gallop. The room around me blurred as I whirled faster and faster around, chasing and being chased by my whirling self. When the walls of my coop spun apart in pieces and room became a blur of ruins, the night seized its chance to swamp my coop. I choked on the thing in my mouth, then wavered, stumbled and fell.

CHAPTER TEN

I awoke spitting water.

My coop was flooded. When I stood up, dung, matting and gobs of snarled hair floated around my ankles. My mat was entirely submerged under water. I looked up to see the early morning sunlight streaking through the thin cracks of the sideboards of the coop.

At first I thought it had rained during the night; that a great deluge had swamped the kennels. Then I heard a loud pattering sound sweep past on the ground outside. Shortly another torrent of water began thundering against my coop. Water began pouring from the roof while whole sheets of water sprayed through the spaces between the sideboards. I peered through one of the larger cracks and saw Old Smokey standing with a water hose about ten feet away pointing a stream of water directly at my coop. Behind him, marching in a solemn procession toward my coop, strode a delegation of several hounds.

I began trembling with anger. I knew it must be Smokey's day to clean the coops and kennel area. Yet he had never begun so early and he had never washed down outside. He was clearly assailing my coop, probably out of revenge for nipping him last week. When he had brought me my food and saw that the last portion had not been touched, he had nudged me with his foot and shocked me from a peaceful sleep. Half from fright and half from anger, I had nipped at him but had barely gotten his ankle. It was but a minor nip. But since then he had stopped bringing me my ration of meat and meal. But obviously that wasn't enough for him to get even and show who was boss. Now he had to flood my coop as well.

Turning from the scene, I surveyed the inside of my coop. The stuffing from my sopped mat rose to the surface of the water and floated with the rest of the debris. When the water would recede, mites and snout beetles would have a field day invading my coop. The knot-holed floor would never keep them out. The place would take at least a week to dry out and the vermin and putrid smell might never leave.

My refuge was no longer.

The more I thought about Smokey, the more intense became my anger. He was as much a part of the kennel world as were the hounds that at that very moment were striding toward my coop. I had come to despise him and the others as much as I had come to hate the hare that was not a hare and the chase that was a game of running around in circles. Everything had become intolerable, and the magnificent stupidity of it all had acted on me long enough. Every time I had hoped for something from the chase, it had denied me. And I had been a glutton for its gross outrage too long. Yet, it had eaten on me only because I had allowed it to. When I asked for something it didn't have to give, I was being my own tormentor. Why not deny the chase as it had denied me? Only when the chase is destroyed will all of the hounds stop hungering for a hare that does not exist.

I splashed through the water and stalked from the coop.

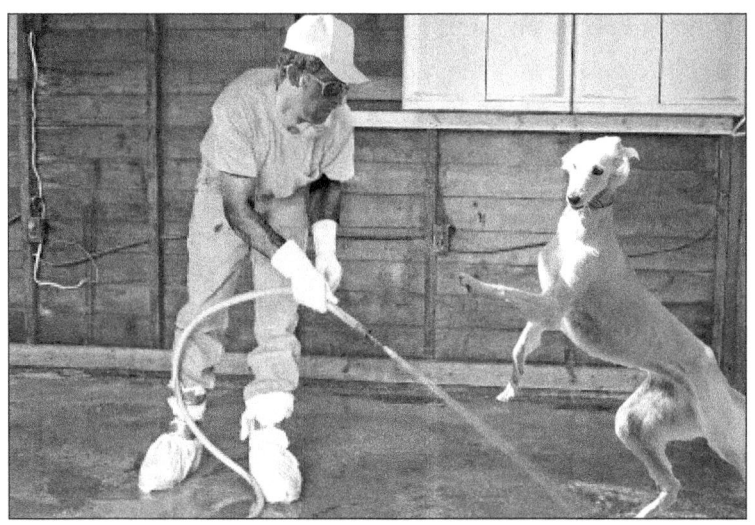

The red sunrise and a huddle of harried looking hounds greeted me as I came striding through the door, ready for anything. I brushed past them without a glance and broke into a run toward Old Smokey. Sprinting around the corner, I skidded—nearly falling in the mud, then caught my balance and caught the clowning kennel keeper in my sights.

He held the water hose so that a lazy fountain arched high into the air and splattered on top of my coop. I barked fair warning, then snarled and advanced a full gallop. He stood as if paralyzed, the water hose now quivering violently in his hand and sending broken jets of water spitting from the nozzle. As I ran toward him, his face twisted into a frightened grimace. I felt exhilarated for the first time in weeks. I felt as though I had gnawed away an entire carcass and found a single choice bone, a bone that became my lost quarry, and a quarry that—if human—at lease was something I could get my teeth into.

I bore down on him.

Four yards away, I sprang into the air and aimed my fore-paws at his chest. Old Smokey looked wild and spooked, then came suddenly alive. He spun around and shot me full on with the water hose. The powerful stream slammed full force into my brisket, staggered and checked me in mid-air, then sent me sprawling to the soppy ground.

Then Smokey dropped the water hose and began running.

The water hose turned and twisted and flailed around until it wedged snugly against a stone. I had fallen into a pool of mud. When I tried standing, my legs slipped out from under me. I couldn't get any traction and watched in helpless fury as Smokey disappeared around the corner of a distant coop. Each time I rose, I slipped, then fell again and again.

The other hounds gathered around the fringe of the puddle. Self-repulsed, I lay fuming in the mud. I was unable to cope with even the slightest situation—unable to complete anything I began and unable to look myself squarely in the eye. Forward Cheque, noble hound that once I was, had become a mere mongrel in the mud.

I wondered why the hounds had come to see me. Their continued silence was uncommonly solemn. I viewed them more closely: Rainless the Red's proud, lean neck was unusually drooped, as if humbled and the Queen of Suir's grey-blue eyes glinted moistly in the early morning sun. Behind them Bonus sat scratching an irksome ear with a restless hind paw. Somewhat beyond stood several other hounds, restlessly pawing the ground and shuffling around.

With difficulty and deep sadness, the Lady Suir informed

me that Saint-Harry had been found dead that morning. The night before he had been seen growing more and more trouble about something he chose not to share with the rest. When the talks adjourned for the evening, the hounds could see that his discontent had frothed into a seething agitation. Later in the night he had been heard yowling like a hound gone mad. He was then seen leaping over the high fence that separated the kennel area from the track. Running straight to the bas-relief, he apparently tried to lift the broken marble slap in which the image of a hare was carved. By wedging his head and neck underneath, he somehow managed to raise the huge mass of stone on its edge. Then Harry slipped on the dewed ground beneath the marble hare and the monstrous stone tipped over and crushed him beneath.

They waited for my response but after I greeted their news with silent indifference, they shook their heads and walked slowly away.

The mud had dried into lumps and hung heavily from my coat. I dragged myself back into the coop. The water had receded and left an old bone on the sleeping mat. I picked it up and lay myself down in its place. I chewed and thought, gnawing at the thoughts that chewed on me, eating them but not tasting what I ate.

The news of Saint-Harry's didn't grieve me. I felt much the same as when the old Colonel had collapsed: despairing but resentful, and quietly outraged by the way things were. It wasn't that a particular hound had died, or even Harry my friend, but rather it was the fact that death was possible— impossible, in fact, to avoid. No, I really didn't mourn for the losses of the Colonel Flash or Saint-Harry. I mourned the loss of life. To think that a hound's breath could be stopped so easily, either by old age or accident; to think that not breathing was not only unavoidable but totally unreasonable as well; and to think that, at prime's peak, it could make me feel as old an aged hound, as old as legend itself.

I bit down hard on the bone. It cracked loudly between my jaws and splintered. A large bone sliver lodged in the gums between my teeth. I tried probing it out with my tongue for a time, then stopped when I tasted blood. Closing my mouth tightly, I sucked hard on the bone, but it would not budge.

And whatever did it mean to stop breathing? A hound that didn't breathe was denied everything: misery as well as happiness. If not breathing was nothing, breathing must therefore be something. Yes, chasing might be a senseless game, but didn't chasing mean more than not chasing?

Must it mean something to be something? A vague but

familiar chasm appeared in my mind's eye. On one side, the chase simply was, but on the other, amidst some flurried cloud, the chase was something else, something more than it appeared to be, but my thoughts clouded as the bone sliver wedged in my teeth became more troublesome. I tried clawing it loose with my paw nail, but it had become seated deep in my gums. Once again raw anger began surging within me. But then a strange thing took place.

The rage, instead of possessing me as before, swelled and matured into pure wrath. As quietly as the water had receded from my coop, and as surely as the mud had hardened on my coat, a change occurred within me. The hate that had crept like frenzied maggots in my belly was slowly transformed into a solitary worm. It fed on itself, growing large, becoming whole. One beast, one mouth, one hunger. My scattered hatred had unified and become something solid. And from it I sensed a welcomed strength. Hate without passion. A calculating rage to cope with the outrage of the chase. I had long before realized the folly of chasing as if the hare were real, as if there were something beyond, but for the first time I realized the possibility of chasing in spite of the fact that the hare was a thing, in spite of the fact that there was nothing beyond. Yes, now I could accept the chase the way it was instead of the way I wanted it to be, but I would do so on my own terms.

I stopped probing for the sliver of bone in my teeth. With pleasure I swallowed the blood that had been filling my mouth, then I sucked for more blood and clamped my jaws together to force the bone deeper into my gums. Pain throbbed from my mouth, radiated exquisitely into my head, and kept swelling until it filled my entire body with a snake of silent scorn. Once more I had a quarry. I knew the quarry would never be mine to catch and conquer, but neither would I be its defeated and destroyed hound.

Let the thing run, I would follow in pursuit, and we would stale mate in the chase.

CHAPTER ELEVEN

I ran in the first event of the day.

Mr. Seth had gaped at me in surprise when I strode resolutely into the grooming room and, with patient defiance, had poised myself proudly in my abandoned stall. He sensed my calm determination, examined me closely, then fetched the grooms, who grumbled loudly as they bathed and curried my coat, cut my lengthened hair and trimmed my ragged nails. They cut burrs and mud lumps from my coat and chased a snout beetle halfway up my nose until their forceps pinched him flat. No doubt annoyed at my haggard condition, they handled me roughly. But their displeasure seemed to give more strength to my increasing contempt. The other hounds passed by my stall, first gawking in disbelief, then croaking with excitement. I looked upon them with a mixture of envy and disdain, and tried to think of other things.

The grooms finished and sighed wearily, were walking proudly around me to admire their handiwork. They slapped a chasing collar around my throat and cinched it tight enough to cause my breathing to become hoarse. Then they hooked me on a leash and led me to the grooming mirror.

The full image of myself burst forth from the slick, glinting surface. Never before had I reflected such a striking stature. I wanted to regard myself longer in the mirror, but the grooms were impatient. They jerked me away and I left

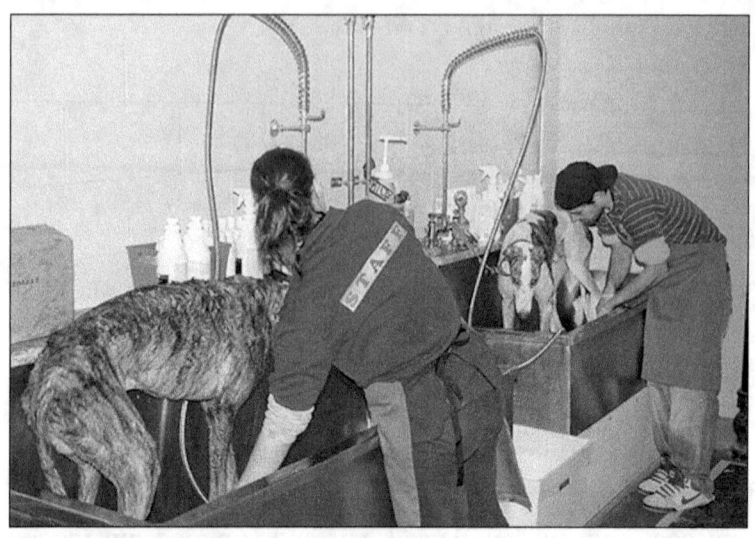

my image behind. They pulled the leash taut against the already tight collar, but their choking inspired me still more. I walked slower than they wanted when we left the grooming room and marched through the passage that tunneled beneath the stadium. They jerked on the leash and I followed: not because they commanded, but because I chose to obey.

The six-hound parade emerged from the passage and strode in single file into the stadium. I knew none of the other five hounds, which were perfect strangers. As entries in the day's first event, we crossed the track and strutted onto the soft turf infield in order to perform the opening ceremony for the early spectators.

The sun bore down on my back. It heated my coat beneath the chasing jacket. I looked upward and matched it eye to eye. Beyond the far end of the stadium, Hoop Mountain rose unclearly from behind a solitary cloud. A dense haze filled the murky blue sky. The spongy turf felt good under my paws and brought me back to the ground.

Music with a slow and steady beat began effusing from the loudspeakers. The grooms paraded us outside the Winner's Circle. The music volume increased. We filed inside the circle of low hedges and tripods overflowing with colorful fresh flowers. Strutting around the circuit with great pride and circumstance, we stopped and turned to face one another in the standard show hound stance. The music crashed and quit. For an instant, silence struck the stadium. Then a talking voice burst from the loudspeakers followed by someone singing. Something bumped inside my belly and I noticed that my leash had slackened. I broke formation and stepped to the center of the Winner's Circle. To the astonishment of all who watched, I hunched, strained and deposited an enormous snake of scorn right before their eyes.

I was quickly ushered to the starting trap.

The Bell, the thing, the doors flew open:

I lunged ahead. My hind feet nearly overtook my fore-feet. I was three long strides out front before the others had even left the starting trap.

Breath came hard at first, but that seemed to spur me all the faster. My tail taunted the pack that galloped behind me. The thought of their surprise enthralled and urged me on. The stadium crowd noted my sudden lead and screamed an early encouragement. The sun had fled behind the solitary cloud that had blown away from old Hoop, and the mountain lay clear and exposed.

I shot out of the first turn.

Never before had my limbs possessed such strength. I cared neither for style nor for saving myself. There was no caution in my gait. Without a single reservation I felt committed to each second as it passed. There was nothing behind me and nothing ahead. The truth lay in the forward movement of each passing moment.

I lagged coming out of the second turn.

A muzzle bumped, then rubbed against my thigh. I glanced around and saw a giant black stud nudging up along the inside. I edged over slowing to the next lane. He advanced until he was almost up with me. I thrust my shoulder square into the lean jackal's neck. He howled, stumbled and fell. Behind me I heard cries of surprise as he bowled into the pack.

Again, I led the chase.

But somehow that was not enough.

I drove myself viciously forward. I thrashed at my legs with my thoughts. They responded and I surged even further

ahead. I all but flew along the backstretch and my strength seemed to increase with my speed. The distance separating me from the fleeting thing was less than it had ever been before. The bone sliver made its presence known. I winced, then ground my jaws together, and the pain became pleasure.

Nearing the three-quarter turn: each gallop out-galloped the last. My lungs had never been fuller. Head down and breathing deeply, I drove myself even harder. I began to notice the stadium crowd. I had never heard them so loud, yet they grew louder still. I wondered what was wrong and looked up.

There, not three feet from my muzzle, bobbed the tail of the thing. Up down, up down, up down, it taunted me right before my nose, and I was convulsed with a sudden rage never before known. My muscles tightened, my wind expired and something thumped in my head. I urged myself onward

and gained a half-step. Now rounding the third turn, the bas-relief caught the corner of my eye. The fallen Colonel fell to mind. I gained a foot more. Saint-Harry's head crashed into sight. Another foot. The thing hopped right before my nose. I strained my neck and got into rhythm with its bobbing bottom. I curled my lips and bared my teeth, then stretched even further forward.

In a flash, as if pulled by an invisible string, despite its already incredible pace, the thing whirred and shot rapidly ahead some twenty feet.

I stopped, benumbed, in the middle of the track.

The deafening crowd and the blaring sun pressed down on me and I got hold of the truth. The thing had some power of flight as strange as my strength of scorn. It made its own rules, just as I had done, and each of us had played out our own game. I stared across at the bas-relief. Those hounds were trapped for all eternity in their marble tomb. And the broken slab bearing the image of the hare would never be replaced but would lay forever unrepaired only to be finally overgrown by the ever growing earth.

I threw back my head and yowled until my wind was gone, until blackness burst before my eyes.

An image of the broken fence opened in my mind and at the moment I knew I must escape from this madness. Jumping up, I wrenched out of the chasing jacket and began running toward the nearest exit gate. The gate attendant saw me coming and quickly swung it shut. I ran wildly to the next gate, further down the track, but another wall of wire slammed bluntly into my nose. On around the track, gate after gate, they all banged shut to close me in until I had reached all the way back to the starting trap.

Squeezing through the partly open doors, I made for the passage that tunneled beneath the stadium and opened up into the kennels. I evaded the twirling leash of Mr. Seth and darted through the opening into the tunnel. The hounds had crossed the finish line and heard me approaching. Foreseeing my intention, they entangled and tripped up their grooms, then bunched together. Snarling from the strength of one another, they guarded and closed off my passage. I threw myself amidst them. The black stud I had bumped in the chase, warded off my assault, then sank his teeth into my shoulder. Mr. Seth closed in behind me, but I sensed the trap before it closed and I broke away.

Running along the outside track, I was nearly deafened by the thunderous uproar issuing from the crowd and loud-speakers. I galloped alone and unassailed along the lanes of the homestretch. Three attendants appeared holding a large net between them. When I turned to elude them and retrace my steps, I saw another trio moving up behind me. I could go neither forward nor backward. I scanned the wooden wall to my left. It rose up ten feet and slanted slightly inward. I began leaping upward, trying to scale the wall, but a torrent of cushions, bottles and howls of execration hailed down upon me from the stadium crowd. The two trios with nets were now running rapidly toward me, hemming me in between them.

I broke for the infield. Leaping high over the inside track railing, I landed upright on the soft green turf. I dashed off to the left, stopped short, then turned and darted to the right. Not certain of the best direction, I began circling the infield along the railing. The attendants began vaulting over the rail. One by one they appeared and positioned themselves around me in the infield.

Now four trios in all, each stretching a rope net between them, closed in cautiously around me screaming, mad dog, rabid mutt, don't let him bite...

I hurdled over the low hedge surrounding the Winner's Circle and landed in a heap inside. The sweet smell of flowers swept in my flared nostrils and soothed my heaving lungs as several screens of mesh netting appeared in the empty sky above me and descended like a crisscrossed trap upon me.

CHAPTER TWELVE

The next day they drove me up Hoop Mountain.

From the rear of a wire-screen truck they dumped me into a wooded camp halfway to the top. I was released into an indolent world of retired hounds that were kept by a crippled keeper. They called it Hoop Home for Hounds.

The small colony of huts lay nestled between a forest of towering trees behind, filling the downward slope of the mountain. A solid rock wall rose up on one side of the camp and a mountain stream flowed down the other. Looking down the mountain I could barely see the chasing stadium, a life's distance away in the valley below. But the haze and the drifting mountain clouds obscured the view of my past life at the kennel and I saw only the unnatural world of the camp trapped within these natural walls.

At first I thought they would shoot me, a common fate for distempered hounds. I waited expectantly each time the keeper shuffled up to my coop, but each time he would only attend to my needs and leave the same way he had come. As the days passed into weeks and still nothing happened, I realized that my life as I knew it was over but my life now was my own, a terrifying thought that made me increasingly desperate.

One day, hoping he would take vengeance, I snapped

viciously at the kennel keeper and tore off one of his pant legs. But he simply backed away, all hunched with soothing words, and now he treated me kinder than ever. Then, for a time, I had tried listening to the older hounds' tales of their youth, but I became only further depressed. So I kept to myself in my hut, sleeping all day in wait for the night. I arose when the sun went down, then hiked to a spot on the river where I lay on the cool moss of the bank to watch the moon fall off a waterfall.

I drifted from one sunrise to the next. The days seemed as grey as the clouds that hung on the side of the mountain above me. The faint but steady drizzle of rain fell upon me to dull all my senses. The nose I had once prided for its keen sense of smell was just a nozzle to pull in and push out a monotonous stream of air. Only the cold water from the fresh water stream in the canyon alerted and freshened my senses.

I came to hate the dusk as the most intolerable time of

day. Neither the sun nor the moon was either here or there; one lingered as if not wanting to leave and the other refusing to assert itself. If I had a choice, I would have chased the grey from the sky and replaced it with black and white.

Each evening I watched the sun's descent and tried to catch that instant when the day became night. The horizon line would grow gradually indistinct and a sea of shadows began filling the wooded valley below. The lean limbs of leafless trees stretched futilely upward to cling to the sky to avoid drowning in the valley's sea of darkness. An evening breeze, still warmed by the sun's last rays, blew across the forest of pines to remind them of their roots in the ground. Although it was only tree limbs swaying in the wind, the whole world seemed to swoon beneath that monstrous, gloaming sky. With their highest branches still groping upwards, the pine trees finally gave way to the shadowy sky and sank wearily down into the dark valley floor. For a time I wondered if it could get any darker without night falling. Wondered: What was holding up the sun? And as I tried to answer, the sun became a pleasant shadow in my eyes and, all at once, the night crashed down.

I felt relief and rose. I stretched and dipped my back, then ambled through Hoop Camp to the worn but narrow path that would take me to the waterfall. The dark sky loomed above me through a narrow swath in the treetops and, although each tree cast a shadow of its own, the forest was a community of darkness.

My belly felt unusually tight and sour, and my feet were simply something somewhere beneath me, but for some rea-son I felt like walking. In fact, I felt like walking off the

world.

Glancing up through an open-top tunnel of treetops, I saw a friendly cloud hovering directly above me.

I howled hello to the cloud.

In response, the cloud sighed as if weary of it all and asked, where was I going?

When I replied that I was walking off a world, the cloud groaned softly, then called me a foolish hound and asked, didn't I know the world was round? The cloud said I was walking around the world, not off it, but if I wanted off, I could get on the cloud's back and walk off the world.

But, I asked, how could I get up so high?

The cloud motioned to a clearing nearby, outside the forest.

I raced through the trees on a trail and emerged in the open meadow, then ran to the highest point where the moonlight glowed, and looked up.

The cloud was lumbering slowly toward me with an

obvious effort. As it descended into the clearing, a sudden breeze began blowing it back toward the forest. The cloud continued moving toward me, but the wind increased and began scattering the cloud into smaller pieces. Then, as it neared where I stood and only a few feet above me, I leaped in the air to reach its back, but instead of the cloud, I caught hold of empty air and fell tumbling down the side of the knoll and stopped short at the base of a tree. I looked back to where my friend the cloud had been, but only the black night looked back.

I lay down and leaned my head against the tree trunk to catch my breath. I felt unhappy about the cloud and wished it would have been my ride off the world. It occurred to me that whomever had a foothold on this earth knew nothing of the whimsy of the wind, but the thought wearied me, so I closed my eyes.

As I slumbered, it seemed the tree bent over and, tapping my shoulder, ordered me off its roots. I jumped up and ran a short distance away but when I turned to glare and challenge it, the tree paid no mind to me. I thought to sneak up and nip the tree's trunk, then dash away, but the short grasses beneath my feet suddenly felt sharp and began pricking my paws. But before I could stomp on the grass and tramp them down, some ferns began flailing my hocks and a stout twig jabbed my forepaw nail. I jumped on the trunk of a fallen tree nearby and had barely caught my breath when the log moaned and rolled over. I fell backwards into a thicket and, scrambling free, I began barging through the forest and filling the still night with the sounds of breaking underbrush and howls of aloneness.

A yellow light flashed through the timber far ahead. I ran toward it, thinking at first it was the rising moon, then I saw it was not only too small, but it blinked on and off as well. As I ran toward it I knew I had to get out of a world before I got off one.

I wound through the brush and trees, leaped over a log, then shuddered and stopped. On a low branch and in full wingspread perched an owl that glared at me with a single yellow eye.

He boldly asked for my destination.

I could not, so I did not reply.

With his shoulders hunched, he blinked his eye and hooted that he had heard me stumbling through the forest and knew I had either lost my way or did not have a way. There was a way, he offered, though only one, but that I would have to trust him to find it.

Then, with a screech that erected my ears, the owl pulled down his wings and lifted himself, circled around me once, then flew off into the denser forest.

I turned and ran the opposite way.

I galloped forward, plunging wildly through the tangles of the forest floor, heading toward what I hoped was the river. I ran until I spotted a hare in the mossy hollow of a fallen tree. As I veered toward him and increased my speed, the creature scampered through the rotted tree trunk, then spurted out the other end and began hopping toward the river for its life. Behind me I heard the owl's wings billowing back through the trees, his wings assailing the air, and I fled after the hare.

The forest exploded to life. Winged things flew up from

the trees and rodents ducked into their holes in the ground. Beasts of all sizes scurried away in wonder and fear of the strange chase in their woods. I ran from the owl and after the hare, wondering who was the quarry and who was the hound.

I soon broke from the forest and, met with the edge of the river, I pulled up. Surrounded by water on three sides, the hare stood on the edge of a narrow patch of land jutting toward the river and cowered fearfully into himself. I heard the owl behind me and caught my breath, then set myself and lunged.

The owl swooped out of the forest and snatched the hare from beneath me, then soared away with its dangling prey while I, stunned by the loss, splashed headlong into the river and was swept rapidly downstream to the distant waterfall.

I struggled desperately at first to reach the bank, then wondered why and gave myself up to the raging torrent. Although I was tossed up and down and turned round and

around, the water way seemed like a natural way. On the land I had found nothing to stand on and nothing to eat. I had walked in circles without taking a step forward, and I had chewed on many things without filling the hunger in my belly. Yes, perhaps the river is the logical way for me and a waterfall the logical end.

The river widened and slowed as I neared the calm edge of a world. The moon beamed brightly on the place where the water cascaded into a peaceful pool below. I lazed in the slow current for a while longer, paddling just enough to keep my head above water, as the water swirled gently around me, soothing my frazzled self.

I thought of the cloud and the owl. A hound had no place in the forest and, surely, he had none in the air. Theirs were not ways for a hound. A hound's way was chasing a hare, yet the river was not a hare, so how could it be the way? But was being without a way better than not being at all?

I clawed at the water and began paddling toward the nearest bank. As I came to the edge, I tried grasping hold of the rocks in the shallows, but each time the current gently swept me from the smooth river stones. When the river offered no help, I realized I had to get out by myself. As I struggled to grasp hold of something solid on the bank, I felt curiously elated by the effort. My feet finally sank into some soft sand and my footing grew steadily firmer. I caught hold of some roots of a washed out tree and pulled myself out of the river and onto the bank.

Tired and broken, unsure whether it was day or night, I collapsed on the ground and then, as time washed by quietly in the river, I found sweet sleep.

When I awoke the moon lay in its descending path to the west. I stood up and shook the last lingering image of the fantasy from my head. Fine mist from the waterfall had sprayed and covered me. I licked off the cool moisture from my coat. Feeling stiff and cold, but curiously awake, I wished I could step out of myself with the same ease as a snake sheds its skin.

I started to return to the camp, and then hesitated. My belly was growling with hunger, which surprised me, for I had long ago stopped longing for food. I went to the edge of the stream dropped my head and lapped at length.

After drinking my fill, I rolled over on my back and stretched my legs in the air. The cold water had aroused my senses and the waterfall sounded louder in my ears. Below, the stream's rippling waves appeared uncommonly distinct as they radiated outwardly and washed fatefully into the bank. And then I smelled something other than evergreen lingering nervously in the air.

My eyes followed my nose down from the base of the waterfall, beyond the calm pool, then along the river bank as it wound downstream, where my eyes then snagged something on the opposite side. There, on a broken tree limb, with the river to its front and the rising mountain behind, sat a fluffy white hare with perked ears and a twitching pink nose. I shook my head, thinking it was another fantasy lingering within, but when I looked again, the creature was still there.

A dreadful hope turned over within me.

I wanted to either remain where I stood or return to my hut in the camp. So far old Hoop Home had been good to me, for there I had forgotten the nightmare of chasing a creature and catching a thing. Anymore, the only things I chased were the lice in my coat. But I sensed the hare on the far bank was not like the thing on the track nor the one in my mind; it could be a real hare, and my gnawing belly urged me forward.

I stalked quietly downstream to a shallow place where the river widened. The wind blew toward me so I had the advantage of smelling the hare without it smelling me. Placing each step carefully before taking the next, I slowly waded across the stream to the bank, then began stalking toward it. My thoughts were confused and I wondered what it was I was doing. My belly replied with a continuous, hollow growl.

The bank between the forest and stream was narrow; I wound slowly through the brush entanglements, and then stopped behind a thick bush to observe the creature more closely.

It sat perched upright with its long ears tilted slightly forward. A short, cocked tail budded proudly from its rump and, although its eyes looked too small for its body, its large nose perfectly fitted its head.

My calmness surprised me as I stepped quietly into the open and walked right up to it. The hare froze, motionless. I stopped at the base of the stump not two feet away and strained my neck for a better smell of it. Snaring his baffled eyes on mine, I pushed out my nose until it sniffed just inches from his warm and furry body. Its scent threw my nose into ecstasy and my belly rumbled anew. The creature rose up on his haunches and, to my surprise, for a moment, leaned curiously toward me.

Then, in a flash, the hare leaped from the stump and hopped rapidly up the mountain slope.

Its flight was so natural I was taken aback. It had already disappeared into the thick woods, but its strong scent stayed behind to tug at my nose. I bounded into the woods in hungry pursuit.

The mountainside was steeper than it looked. The hare hopped no faster than the thing on the track, but it ran in a much different course. Instead of running straight up the mountain, it seesawed up the slope in an angular pattern. I often lost sight of it as it ran astray, then I would hear it rustling faintly in the leaves ahead. After awhile I realized that the easiest way to pursue it was to follow its scent with my nose.

The hare continued weaving back and forth as it hopped higher up the mountain slope. As its scent changed from strong to faint, I followed, then lost, then once again found his winding path. The smell once escaped me altogether and I thought it had gotten free from my chase, but I backtracked the trail and soon found it again. Then the scent grew excitingly strong.

It led me to a tree and then stopped. I dashed beyond but found nothing so I retraced my steps. I circled the area, peering into patches of thickets and briar, but found nothing and returned to the tree. Then I looked up.

The hare sat hovering in the crotch of two limbs that was hanging directly above me. I leaped up, but it huddled just out of my reach, and was as safe as it could be. In frustration, I began barking and running around the base of the tree.

But then a strange noise stopped me. Peering up through the branches, I saw a large owl sitting and staring at me from a tree limb only a few feet above the hare, its two eyes glaring defiantly through the branches. Inspired, I leaped again at the hare, but it scampered up to the higher limb on the next

limb. Screeching, the owl spread its wings and pounced, but the hare scooted under its claws and hopped out to the edge of the limb. The owl flew out of the tree and circled wide to return and snatch up the hare, but as it swooped down, the hare dropped to the ground and fled once again up the mountain. The owl flew back to his tree and I began running after the hare. The first rays of morning sun crept quietly over the mountaintop.

We soon ran out of forest and broke into an open meadow. I guessed this was the top of Hoop Mountain, for the air was thin and I was out of wind. The hare, too, was tiring; it had slowed and I was closing in from behind.

The open ground gave me the vantage. It began using evasive tactics as I drew closer. I lost steps each time it changed pace and swerved, but each time I caught up again. The bright sunrise splashed fully over the top of the mountain and nearly blinded me as the hare feigned left, then

dodged to the right in front of me. I pounced and trapped it under my paws.

At last! I caught the hare!

But the tense cry that squeezed from its throat gave me pause. I had the hare, I had caught it, which was what I had been trained to do, but I had been trained to chase a thing, not a creature, so what did it really mean to trap this small puff of life and hold it prisoner in my paws?

Although it was paralyzed with fear, I could feel the creature's heart pounding wildly against my paws. Its ears were flopped against the sides of its head and its eyes are piercing mine with a fear beyond belief.

I shook my head, trying to make some sense of this small puff of fur between my paws shuddering in fear, while I stood over it pondering its and my fate. What about its fate? And what about mine? Where did it come from that a hound had to chase a hare? And where was it said what was a hound to do if ever he caught one?

I relaxed my pressure on the hare, and when it sensed the possibility of freedom, it struggled to get free from my grip. But it was trapped—just as I was, but what was the trap? Was it simply that I was a hound and it was a hare? That I just wanted to chase it and it just wanted to elude me?

And then it struck me: I wanted to catch it while it only wanted to be free. There could only be one winner.

Yet, by trapping it, was it imprisoning me with the idea of chasing and catching it? Any chase? Any catch? Any hare?

So, am I trapped by the simple act of chasing? And is chasing nothing more than a monstrous idea? Likewise, is the hare fated to being chased? Then it seemed to me that both the hare and the hound only want to be free, or at least have the freedom to feel free.

Yes, to feel free! That was it! And neither hound nor hare wanted to be duty bound to chase or be chased.

I looked again at the small creature between my paws,

If I wanted the same thing as this fluff of life in my grips, why should I deny it the very thing I want?

I had chased and I had caught. But why and what had I caught? Just what was it lying here on the ground between my paws? It's everything I had always expected: it is soft and breathes; it ran like the wind and smelled like some wild thing in my snout. It wasn't the thing from the track or a thing in my head, and yet it meant nothing more or less than anything else. I had chased and caught another something and gotten another mouthful of nothing. The hare I had long sought I had finally caught, and though real, it meant really nothing.

I poked gently at the little thing and its whole being changed from being a fear-ridden creature to an angry animal: its eyes now glared at me and its body tensed as if defying my power to take its life away while I, feeling full well the power of having its fate within my paws, suddenly felt ashamed of myself for terrifying this small fluff of life.

Without thinking what I did, I released my hold on the hare and let it lie freely where it was on the ground. When it did not move, I thought I may have harmed it, but upon realizing I meant no further harm, in an instant the creature jumped up and hopped quickly into the nearby underbrush.

I looked up. I was at the top of Hoop Mountain where I could see the clouds above me and, far below, I could barely make out the kennels and oval chasing track. Between them I saw a forest of swaying trees surrounding the lower mountain and a peaceful river meandering down its side.

Here I was: Standing with my chin in the clouds on the upmost peak of the mountain. I stood at the top of a world. The scene absorbed me for a time, then once again I became aware of the bone sliver in my mouth. I sucked on it hard, as I had done for weeks, but this time it came loose and I spat it from my mouth, at once freed from the nagging pain I had pushed into myself.

As I peered at the peaceful scene around me, all alone and above it all, I wondered, what in the world was I really chasing? Was I my own hare as well as my own hound?

I lay down for a moment and closed my eyes to the morning.

Was the answer to forget everything else and chase after the hare inside myself? But does that make any more sense

than anything else?

No. Of that I was certain. No, it made no sense.

I had listened to old Colonel Flash and had chased as a hope-hound. I had curled up in anger and had scorned the world as a hate-hound. Then as a head-hound I had gotten lost in a forest of fancies.

I had chased the hope as if the hare were real; I chased the hate even when I knew it wasn't real; and then I chased the dreams when it seemed they were all that was left to chase. And now I had chased and caught the real thing, a living hare, and still nothing I did seemed to satisfy the curious hunger that gnawed deeply within me.

Was there no hare to hound? No hound to chase?

But how can a hound live in the world without a hare? Is it possible?

Was the hound destined simply to chase? Was harehounding the hope, or could such a thing be done?

I raised myself and stood up, then reared back my head and howled until my lungs gave out; it was a pleading sound offered to all but was lost in the wind and heard by none. I turned and looked squarely at the crimson rays of sun now splashing over the top of Hoop Mountain. The sunrise looked like a spray of bright flowers bursting joyously from the east. I felt the fresh morning sun filling me with warmth and expectation, though of what I was unsure.

Turning once more, I peered down at the steep, descending slope, then hesitated, sensing both fear and vague excitement.

Then, feeling strong and curiously calm—and without one backward glance—I began zigzagging forward down the mountainside with the multi-colored sunrise glowing warmly behind me and the thought of new places spreading before me, places where I could run and play to explore and discover my newly found freedom to feel free.

THE END

DEDICATION

The late Bernard Malamud (1914-1986), along with Saul Bellow and Philip Roth, dominated Jewish literature in America during the 1960's and 1970's.

As a pre-dental student in 1957, my curriculum required taking a liberal arts course. I enrolled in Mr. Malamud's creative writing class and, by the second year, to my surprise, he invited me—a goy—to be his first ever, private tutorial student, an honor that humbles me to this day. I have often thought about the inscription he wrote to me in one of his novels: "All good things, including maybe writing?"

I had enrolled in dental school but, upon discovering that looking into people's mouths was not my forte, I quickly resigned and returned for a degree in literature. At Mr. Malamud's suggestion, and notwithstanding his recommendation, I received a fellowship to the Writer's Workshop in Iowa City where, after studying everything written by and written about the existentialists, Camus, Kafka, Sartre and Hesse, I wrote *Harehound* in 1962, which I call an existential fable.

Now, after fifty years of being an educator, craftsman and businessman, I have returned to my writing, but I have never forgotten Mr. Malamud's inscription. Nor have I forgotten the hero of his first book, *The Natural,* Roy Hobbs, who as the rookie who struck out Babe Ruth enroute to the majors, mysteriously disappears only to reappear many years later to become a baseball hero, who was memorialized by actor Robert Redford in a movie of the same title.

I am forever grateful to my mentor and it is to him that I modestly dedicate this novela.   —*Gary M. Koeppel, 2012*

THE AUTHOR

Gary M. Koeppel

Gary M. Koeppel grew up in Albany, Oregon, a small town in the Willamette Valley and, as a boy, spent his summers visiting his great aunt and uncle, a Coast Guard Captain and Keeper of the Heceta Head lighthouse on the Oregon Coast. At night his aunt would peel apples in her rocking chair in front of the fireplace as she told spellbinding stories about their adventures while tending lighthouses on the Pacific Ocean along the Northwest coast. It is from her he credits his imagination.

Koeppel's parents, whose grandparents emigrated from Switzerland, endured and survived the Great Depression. At age 14 Koeppel's father, Carl, the eldest of a large family, was asked by his father to leave home because he could not feed him. He moved to Chicago where he lived in the YMCA and, for money, he sang and tap-danced on bar tops in beer halls during lunch hours for pennies in tips. At 16 he joined thousands of Hobo's who worked—not begged—for food as they rode the rails across America until he arrived in Oregon, a place he called "God's country."

Koeppel's mother, Barbara, had a scholarship to become a teacher but, when her father abandoned her mother and six brothers and sisters, she sacrificed her career to work as a grocery store clerk and to care for her younger siblings. Her brother was a dental technician who trained Carl whom she later married and became his dental assistant. She also became an accomplished porcelain ceramicist.

While studying pre-dentistry in college, Koeppel needed a required liberal arts course and signed up for a creative writing class taught by Bernard Malamud, a renowned Jewish-American author, whose influence on him was soon realized.

Koeppel was accepted into the dental school but dentistry did not suit him, so he quickly left and returned to undergraduate school for a degree in literature. With a letter of recommendation from his writing mentor, Malamud, he received a graduate fellowship to the prestigious Writer's Workshop in Iowa City where Koeppel earned his way providing research for workshop founder Paul Engler and where he wrote his first novel, *Harehound.*

But instead of publishing the book and becoming a writer, Koeppel was fearful that he had nothing to write about, so for the next seven years he taught writing and European literature as an English professor at universities in Iowa, Puerto Rico and Oregon. At Portland State University he developed a new method of teaching writing, which he called 'Experiential Composition' that involved assigning experiences to students they had to undertake and then write about in the first person to him as the audience.

In 1967 at Portland State University, Koeppel also produced the country's first university-accredited program on the subject, *LSD and the Psychedelic Movement* featuring guest appearances by Timothy Leary, Alan Watts, Allen Ginsburg, Ken Kesey, The Merry Pranksters, and Doctor Samuel Irwin, a psycho-pharmacologist from the University of Oregon Medical School. Koeppel served as the university president's counselor to the freshman class on drug use and abuse.

In 1968 Gestalt psychiatrist Fritz Perles of Esalen Institute in Big Sur, California, learned of Koeppel's innovative teaching methods and invited him to teach writing to Esalen seminarians. However, due to the paranoia and psychosis caused by the drug culture of the 1960's, Koeppel left Esalen and moved to Malibu where—at first as a hobby, then professionally—he developed a new kind of sand candle, became an American craftsman and wrote a book for Chilton titled *Sculptured Sandcast Candles.*

As "K the Kandler" he carved candles in malls throughout California, then at Universal Studios and Disneyland. As his candles became successful, he returned to Big Sur and bought the Coast Gallery in 1971, but two years later the gallery was inundated by a flood that was exacerbated by a 100-year storm. To recover he designed and rebuilt the gallery by recycling large, municipal redwood water tanks into an in-the-round complex that has become a historic architectural landmark on the Big Sur Coast. In 1978, to stop an attempt to federalize Big Sur as a National Park, he founded and published the *Big Sur Gazette* newspaper. As in David and Goliath, the Big Sur citizenry won the battle for Big Sur, and he learned the ancient lesson that the pen is more powerful than the sword.

During the next 30 years Koeppel and his wife, Emma, opened art galleries in Maui, Pebble Beach and Carmel while producing 30 Global Art Expos in Japan, Israel, Germany, Hawaii, New York and California. He became Henry Miller's art dealer during the last 10 years of Miller's life and continues to be his posthumous art publisher and licensing agent.

By 2012 Koeppel had divested himself of his art galleries and art expos, and returned to writing—exactly 50 years after writing his first novel, *Harehound.* He has just finished rewriting an incomplete manuscript written by Lillian Bos Ross titled *The Road,* which is the third book of the recently published *Big Sur Trilogy.*

He is currently writing a book about Edgar Haber, an American entrepreneur who created a golfing oasis and a five-star hotel out of a cow pasture, the working title for which is *The Golf Legend of Quail Lodge.*

His next book is an investigative exposé about the mortgage derivatives fiasco created by bankers-turned-brokers, an illegal and monstrous money racket that has destroyed multitudes of American dreams of home ownership, bankrupted America's mortgage market and burdened homeowners with untold financial miseries for decades to come. The working title of this investigative bombshell is *How to Beat the Bank and Keep Your Home.*